ALSO BY TREVOR TUCKER

Ned Kelly's Son

A saga of Australian heritage... almost lost in history.

The Stolen Maps:

Australia's greatest maritime secret?

Aussie Anecdotes

A collection of quintessential Australian short stories.

A SENSE OF JUSTICE

A TALE OF RETRIBUTION FOR TWO UNLIKELY
AUSTRALIAN HEROES

TREVOR TUCKER

TREVOR TUCKER PUBLISHING

First published 2022 in Australia by Trevor Tucker Publishing
Copyright © Trevor Tucker 2022
All rights reserved
www.trevortuckerpublishing.com.au

A Sense of Justice
EPUB: 978-1-922825-06-3
POD: 978-1-922825-07-0

Cover design by Leandra Wicks

In memory of Beau Dickinson: an Australian cattleman, drover and great friend who had a fascination with "characters of the olden days" and a belief that justice, even that of "simple bush justice", would always prevail over evil.

1

———————

Gazing through the bars of the cell, the turnkey could easily be forgiven for thinking that the scruffy and unshaven, but otherwise handsome young man lying before him on a threadbare mattress was on his deathbed.

By reputation and deeds, this prison guard was generally devoid of compassion and usually could not have cared less; he'd seen thousands of men pass through this bleak place. He also knew for certain that either a lethal dose of pleurisy or the gallows awaited some and that another kind of death awaited most of the others: their fate... transportation to a Godforsaken location on the other side of the world and then, if they survived that voyage, needing to somehow endure the ongoing loss of their freedom for the next seven years.

Even so, the guard's interest was genuinely aroused on this occasion. To him this lad's posture was surprising—bizarre in fact—for he had never previously witnessed anyone in his care who had held such a self-satisfied look of resignation as that now on this young man's face... despite the cell's filthy, freezing flagstone floor and fetid surrounds.

"

Had the guard then concluded that this was probably another way of dealing with the inevitability of impending death, he would have been wrong. Looks, after all, can be deceiving.

Oblivious to his surroundings and discomfort, eighteen-year-old Harry Taylor simply lay on his back contemplating the harrowing events which had so devastatingly upheaved his otherwise stable and secure life during the past six months.

* * *

As an innocent young boy Harry loved exploring his surroundings and ranged far and wide in doing so. During these jaunts he engaged in many daring, childish, fun activities, which, much to his annoyance and inability to understand why, occasionally landed him in trouble. The consequences back then had been nothing more than a stern word from his father on "doing what you're told" or "how to look after yourself".

As Harry approached adulthood, he applied himself to a variety of jobs, becoming adept at every task he took on and had a reputation as a reliable, likeable, polite and hard-working lad.

However, when provoked, Harry never took a backward step and mastered another bent... that of very efficiently stopping fights, not starting them. For this talent, his father, though secretly proud of his son's ability to look after himself, would lecture Harry "to pull your head in son. Just walk away, or one day you'll land yourself in real strife". But that advice never sat well with Harry.

Regardless, whatever punishment then followed, it was never as pointless or inconceivably cruel as what he was now forced to endure.

* * *

Dear God, if there is one, why was I born English? Harry struggled desperately with this question many times during the initial four months of his incarceration in the Coldbath Fields Prison in Clerkenwell, London, one of England's most notorious, stinking, vermin-infested, brutal and overpopulated prisons.

But strangely, Harry was becoming increasingly more disciplined, self-assured and determined. This, he intuitively and rightly understood, was the only possible human survival response to being continuously deprived of privacy or human interaction, manacled by hand and foot, always cold, on the verge of starvation and without either full daylight or the slightest zephyr of fresh air.

* * *

THE UNFATHOMABLE UNFAIRNESS of this "English justice" constantly frustrated and haunted Harry, for he had simply removed from a building site (albeit after dark) a three-foot length of flat timber that appeared to be a discarded off cut; an item he desperately needed to complete the coffin he had been constructing for his recently deceased, much-loved father.

However, that need was overridden by a self-important citizen who happened to be strolling past the building site and who found great delight in reporting Harry to the police that night, insisting that *"the consequences arising from a citizen's civic duty to report such actions must prevail over any notion that profiting from stolen goods could be tolerated in England"*.

The owner of the building site was easily coerced into laying theft charges. After all, as that upright citizen pointed out to him, *"surely it's your duty to support someone who was acting in your best interests"*. Had the building site owner not pressed charges, the public's perception of that "citizen" would have diminished significantly, and so to avoid being made to look stupid, a "donation" exchanged hands—just enough to sway the building owner's decision to lay the charges that would seal Harry's fate.

Of course, in front of the judge, the words of that wealthy, self-opinioned "witness" carried far more legal weight than a destitute Harry Taylor could provide without the services of a smart solicitor. (The witness had from the outset of the court hearing cleverly and emphatically categorised Harry as *an unemployed, impudent lout*: a patently wrong description, for Harry was neither of those things.) Nevertheless, the witness had cold-bloodedly employed this tried-and-true tactic to make the job of his regular drinking friend, an overworked judge, less demanding.

Clearly the judge cared not a jot for either Harry's emotional state or his plead for leniency, and so, in the absence of legal counsel, Harry's attempt to re-establish his bona fides were unworthily and shamefully disregarded by the tired judge— the result being that Harry was now scheduled for "Transportation". The judge, when summarising his decision explained that in applying the law, precedents, above all else, had to be followed.

Also, irrationally, and grossly unfair in Harry's opinion, there was no obligation for the English Government to provide financial assistance to his family, which had just lost the guiding influence of his father and now himself, the family's only legal bread winner. This realisation ravaged Harry's conscience, for there was now *absolutely nothing* he could do about this absurd situation... one so trivial in its origin.

A judicial appeal would not be tolerated, nor could it have been afforded anyway. There were no wealthy relatives or friends who could help... the only recourse for his family now being illegal pursuits necessary just to stay alive. In other words, his mother, two sisters and ailing brother had probably each just been delivered their death sentences. And worse, Harry's situation guaranteed that he would never hear from them, or ever see them again.

However, Harry had a plan. He was still strong, despite the dreadful prison food and conditions, for he had youth on his side. But moreover, he'd discovered a new purpose in life. Yes, his plan was selfish in many ways but his need to survive was paramount, which meant if he was going to remain sane, he had to relinquish all family connections and somehow, ruthlessly disregard every emotion associated with that severing. Later, there might be time for memories of family, but only after his plan succeeded.

That plan was indeed cunning despite how implausible it at first seemed to Harry. In his opinion, though the judge had acted slavishly and without compassion in arriving at his ruling, he may also unwittingly have given Harry exactly what he wanted: the opportunity to see the world without ever having to go to war to defend an England he now despised.

* * *

As if a warm clean blanket had just been thrown over Harry, peace had settled upon him; his anger, emotional confusion and grief were now rapidly in retreat and his physical tension was following suit as his body relaxed. He had no idea how long the gentle smile on his face remained in place—or cared—for his primary thought was... *if those fools send me to the other side of the world, it won't cost me a farthing.*

In the early hours of the morning a more sobering thought surfaced from Harry's sub-conscious: *I wonder if I'll ever yearn to return to England?*

Who knows how many days later, keys rattled outside the cell. Shortly after, the guard cautiously pushed open the cell door, allowing muted light to flood the space that had become Harry's loathsome living quarters.

'So what is it, you oaf? Are you here to give me one of your famous beltings?', Harry asked just a little more condescendingly than he intended.

'Just get up, Sunshine. The Guv' wants a word with yah. I'm gunna remove yah leg-irons, an' then I want yah arse up those stairs. An' don't be considerin' any funny business or I'll break both yah legs then kick yah straight back down 'ere.'

Only once since his sentencing had Harry left this cell; a complete surprise only a few weeks previously. For him that outing was a momentous event, which put his survival plan into motion and gave rise to his newfound optimism.

2

<hr>

'Ah yes; thank-you, Hawkins', said the Governor to the prison guard and then quickly added with unmistakeable authority, 'you can leave me alone with the prisoner but wait outside. There's a good man.'

'Now Taylor, we need to talk,' grumbled the Governor as he turned his attention to Harry. Before him stood a mature youth at least six feet tall, long of limb and square of shoulder, his light brown hair unkempt and unclean... and unnervingly blue eyes. Yes, he recognised him, just; altogether a little gaunt, but that was to be expected given the prison food. Nevertheless, a fine example of approaching manhood, someone who the Governor knew would have made this lad's father very proud. 'No, you can't sit. I don't want your stink embedded into my furniture.'

While maintaining a relaxed, attentive stance, Harry courteously nodded his understanding, for he knew he was indeed on the nose. However, his gaze remained fixed upon the Governor's eyes.

'I've been considering your audacious request since we first met; three weeks ago, I believe. I must say, Taylor, it has merit, so listen carefully.

'The rumours you somehow heard about were correct. Due to an ever-increasing number of felons convicted under existing laws, this prison and a hundred or more around our country will soon be enlarged to accommodate many, many more poor souls just like you.

'To punish people for crimes of even less magnitude than yours, our nation's being flooded with prisoners... which *I* believe amounts to treachery being needlessly served upon many unlucky folks. I'm glad that you agree with my views, Taylor.

'You were also correct that there's now considerable opposition from our new colonies to where our felons have previously been automatically transported and then dumped... and rightly so in my opinion. You can't really blame those governors for being sick and tired of us continuing to do that.

'Incidentally, I was officially informed this very morning that our government is finally about to announce the end of future prisoner transportation programs. Presumably, our *infallible* Government believe their prison expansion program will solve all their future prisoner accommodation problems.

'I emphatically reject this flawed development, Taylor but regrettably I'm powerless to alter *any* laws: they just want *a bit each way* and bugger any humanitarian considerations!

'Logically our prison numbers will now continue to grow dramatically, not reduce, yet our "powers that be" still want no immediate change to their overriding objective... to get rid of *all* offenders. Yes Taylor, that includes people like you, as absurd as that is. And if I want to keep my job, I'm now being forced to reduce my prison population as efficiently as possible... *before* transportation is formally abolished!'

Harry shifted his weight and said, 'Mr Galbraith... ah, Governor. I greatly appreciate your frankness and I believe your frustration is genuine. As my life depends on it, I pledge not to betray your views. But sir, where is this conversation going?'

'Be patient for just a few more minutes, young man. And be certain that if I ever hear my words being spoken against me, I'll know their source and I'll have you swinging from the nearest gallows in record time.'

Harry swallowed and shuffled uneasily. 'We are in total agreement then, sir,' he replied confidently, for there was no doubting the menace in the Governor's words.

'I've read the court's notes in your file and admit I was taken by your domestic situation leading to your arrest and subsequent senseless conviction,' Galbraith continued. 'I too lost my father from an untreatable malady; "consumption" the doctors called it. He died a terrible death and he too Taylor, was a good man, just like your father.'

Governor Galbraith's voice was now subdued, his words tumbling out as if he was talking to his own son. 'I have no right, but bugger it, boy, I resolved there and then to assist you in any way possible. Regrettably however, I can't release you Harry, but I can perhaps smooth the way for you.

'Accompanying that Government announcement I mentioned earlier, I received a demand that fourteen of the worst cases in my care are to be prepared for immediate transportation to New Holland.

'Accordingly, I've signed all the documentation for the fourteen of those I consider my worst scoundrels, but what you need to know now is just how lucky you are, son... for I've also accepted your most unusual offer to *volunteer* for transportation. You'll be among the last inmates to leave Coldbath Fields Prison.'

As realisation settled, Harry started to grin, then suddenly his face lit up in an equal measure of surprise and understanding, eyes wide open and open-mouthed. In unison, the Governor smiled broadly.

'Bugger the furniture, Harry, you'd better sit-down lad; we've got much more to discuss. And don't take offence at the need to characterise you as a scoundrel; I for one know that's preposterous. However, I'm sure you'll handle that minor inconvenience of title.

'To answer your earlier question, our government, in its infinite wisdom, has elected not to cancel those transportations previously scheduled. You will therefore be sailing on the *Hougoumont*, which will depart from Portsmouth on the 12th of October. Yes, that's right Harry, it departs in just seven days' time and that'll be the last time any British ship departs our shores as a prisoner transportation vessel.

'Mind you, there are at least four other such ships already at sea, heading for New Holland as we speak. Of course, none of them will have any idea about this development and none will return with their current cargo; that's definite.

'Fortunately, you didn't delay your request for a hearing with me: had you done so, we would not be having this second conversation. A refusal was always on the cards, but regardless, you showed great mettle for which I salute you. However, I can't imagine your chances of surviving another seven years in this soul-destroying place had you missed this opportunity. Can you?'

'Definitely not, Mr Galbraith,' replied Harry, 'I was close to going crazy as it was, Guv.'

'Right then, here's what will happen in the next few days. You will receive from me a letter of my recognition of your good behaviour, usefulness and general helpful conduct while in my care. These remarks will be based upon me having witnessed your legendary carpentry skills and having discussed with you your interest in animal husbandry... though I feel I may be stretching the truth slightly. I'd suggest that you quickly learn as much as you can about both activities. I can't recommend anyone regarding the former, but Hawkins, your esteemed turnkey, was raised on a farm and apparently once owned several horses. I'll have a word with him to answer your questions and set you right on farming matters.'

The Governor stared back at Harry, not quite sure why the lad's expression was so dreamlike. In essence, Harry was dumbfounded by the pace of proceedings and wondering how on earth he could ever repay such consideration.

Regardless, the Governor pressed on. 'To hopefully make it easier for you to find employment in your new country, my letter will also recommend that you be granted a Ticket of Leave as soon as possible upon your arrival; it will state that in my professional judgment you are a person to be trusted: indeed, a worthy volunteer and not a scoundrel.'

'Bloody hell, Mr Galbraith, that's really decent of you,' Harry interrupted excitedly, oblivious that he had just sworn in front of the Governor.

'Just make sure you do *not* lose this letter; your life might depend upon it. I'd also suggest that you endear yourself with the ship's Captain. His name is William Cozens. I know little about him, but if he is a fair-minded individual, he *may* "keep an eye out for you", so to speak: no guarantee of course.'

The Governor then reached behind his chair and produced a medium-sized canvas and leather carry bag which he passed to Harry. 'Now take this and look after it. I know this is most irregular, as are the thirty pennies hidden inside. You'll also find some half decent clothes in there, so make sure you tub up before you put them on. You can't go on board in those stinking rags you're now wearing. And wash your hair.'

'With pleasure, sir,' Harry replied happily, but quickly the expression on his face changed to one of serious concern. 'Do you know much about the ship, Mr Galbraith... or what it'll be like on board?'

'Yes, a little. I know that the *Hougoumont* is referred to as a Black-wall frigate. It has three masts and is fully rigged for sailing. As I said earlier, it will depart from Portsmouth on the 12th of October. There will be two hundred and eighty prisoners and over a hundred passengers on board, which includes the prisoner guards and their families, and several free passengers. I daresay the ship is quite large, but I suspect free space will be at a premium. And oh yes, there will be a surgeon on board.

'I've also been informed that there will be many literate convicts on board, more than usual for a convict ship; something to do with their unacceptable political beliefs.

'I was told only yesterday by our prison librarian that the *Hougoumont* was chartered by the French as a troop carrier during the Crimean War, albeit then it was known as the *Baraguey d'Hilliers*. So it's my guess it would've been easier to convert *it* into a convict ship, rather than others on offer. Regrettably Harry, you're about to discover just how good a job they did, or otherwise.

'Based on previous sailings, apparently it takes about ninety days to travel to the west coast of New Holland. Obviously, that'll depend upon sailing conditions. Once you arrive, you'll be off-loaded at a small community known as Fremantle, where you'll be assigned to a prison cell and again, regrettably, to an uncertain future. It's my belief however, that opportunities abound in that new colony, based on an ever-increasing number of favourable reports which confirm this.

'Well, that's about all I can tell you and do for you, son. Just keep your nose clean if you know what I mean ... and good luck.'

'I'll not forget your consideration and kindness, Mr Galbraith,' said Harry as he thrust out his hand to shake that of his keeper.

'One last word of warning, lad. There will be some nasty and unsavoury individuals accompanying you: murderers, rapists and some totally deranged poor bastards. Stay clear of them all!

'You also need to know that one such person, a huge loathsome beast of a man, is among that lot. His surname is Bickford, but for some reason he calls himself "Brickie". Based on our experience with him here at Coldbath, he'll do everything in his power to get the better of you physically and mentally. If you run into this bastard while on board and he challenges you, summon the guards immediately and let them deal with him. Just make sure that you let those guards know his only weakness; he has an unnatural aversion to water. The only way we've been able to keep him under control is to threaten to throw buckets of cold water over him any time he plays up.

FOR SEVERAL HOURS after the Governor had transferred Harry back into Hawkins' care, Harry was amazed at not only how quickly his plan had progressed... but even more astonished at how the meeting he'd just attended had left his self-belief and confidence soaring.

3

———————

PORTSMOUTH, mid-afternoon, 11th October 1867

'Righto laddie,' the loud, demanding voice of Hawkins boomed as he threw open the cell door and entered Harry's filthy domain. 'C'mon, I want yah arse out of here, you're goin' places. Strip off those rags yah wearin' then grab yah belongin's. You're first off to the ablutions block where I'll see to it yah get a good hosin' down... from head to toe. Well come on, look lively and don't be shy; get naked, son!'

Having stood under a blast of near-freezing water for just a few minutes Harry's skin tingled from the effects of the coarse towel he had been supplied to dry himself with, the relentless parasitic itch that usually inhabited every nook and cranny of his body had now blissfully ceased. He felt exhilarated. And as he flung his long, damp hair back across his head, he also felt gratitude: for the first time in months, his hair didn't stink or feel greasy. As Harry exited the cold ablutions block, he experienced an almost forgotten pleasure from that which came from good fitting footwear, and clean dry clothes.

But of course, there had to be one dissenter during the prisoner pre-departure communal ablutions chore... Brickie! He had initially made a fuss at being asked to wash, and promptly, in a great display of bad temper hurled the contents of his washbasin over one of the guards. He then threw a block of soap at another guard, scoring a direct hit to the poor man's eye. His ongoing barrage of expletives and lack of cooperation only relented when the guards dragged some huge, high volume sluice hoses into the ablution block.

'Righto Harry, the wagon's this way,' Hawkins instructed, his previous gruff voice replaced with sociable camaraderie. 'And I've got some good news for yah, lad.'

'Pray tell, what's that? Perhaps your mates intend to drown Brickie with those hoses... that'd be really good.'

'Nah, better than that. It seems the 'onrable citizen as what dobbed yah in took a terrible hidin' a few nights back. Damn nearly killed the bastard I believe.'

'Bloody hell, who'd do that sort of thing?' Harry chuckled cynically. 'Mind you, it sounds a bit like payback to me.'

'I 'aint sayin, but the Guv's been known to move in mysterious ways.'

Both men laughed jovially then continued their walk side-by-side to the waiting wagon that would deliver Harry and the other prisoners to the docks where the *Hougoumont* was berthed.

Harry stopped walking and lightly grabbed Hawkins by the arm. 'Yah know what Hawkins? When we first met and ever since, I absolutely hated your guts. But you've changed a lot since I had that last meeting with the Governor. In fact, you're not such a bad bastard after all. You've taught me just about everything there is to know about animals and farming... and well, I've come to trust you. Your unexpected news is therefore most welcome: it sort of squares the ledger, so to speak.'

'It does indeed,' Hawkins quietly replied as they continued their walk. 'Well lad, 'ere we are. I'm sorry, but I must cuff yah and fit yah with leg irons when yah get inside the wagon. Them's the rules. Don't worry; they'll not be too tight.'

'Thanks Hawkins, you're only doing your job. I hold no grudges my friend. You know, I think I'm actually looking forward to what beckons.'

'That's good because most prisoners usually start blubberin' or screamin' revenge at this stage.

'Anyway, here, don't forget yah bag and the fifty pennies yah've got tucked away in there.'

'Eh?' replied Harry, astonished. 'What *fifty pennies*? How'd you know I had any money in there?'

'That's for me tah know an' you tah guess, Harry. Most irregular, eh?'

Both men smiled as understanding dawned on Harry's face. They firmly shook hands both knowing they'd never meet again, but thankful they had. 'Thanks again, Hawkins.'

'Good luck, lad. Look after yahself, an' keep yah nose clean... if yah know what I mean, eh?'

4

The ensuing eighty-nine-day voyage to Fremantle included a brief stopover in Cape Town for reprovisioning. However, not all the initial passengers were accounted for when the *Hougoumont* eventually docked in Western Australia on 9th January 1868.

* * *

LIFE AT SEA as a convict had its advantages, the most telling being that of access to ozone-laden and clean fresh air. No longer forced to inhale the ever-pervasive sulphurous odour of mass humanity, all on board reveled in this natural luxury: often chilly but always invigorating.

The second most appreciated benefit was the conditional freedom which Captain Cozens afforded all prisoners; daily release from their below-deck confines, for two hours to exercise—weather permitting—and an opportunity to mingle with the free, unrestricted, paying passengers.

Ordinarily however, prisoners were only permitted to talk with their fellow prisoners, and only provided they gathered in groups of not more than four: armed guards vigorously enforced this. On a rotational basis, only thirty prisoners were ever simultaneously permitted on deck.

Initially, during reprieves from their cells, the prisoners remained shackled by hand and foot. However, over time, as their part of the bargain "not to misbehave" was demonstrated, their shackles were removed. The alternative, if even one prisoner caused either any anxiety, discomfort, or trouble to any free passenger, or committed any act which threatened the safe sailing of the *Hougoumont*, all privileges, to all prisoners would be immediately withdrawn.

Of course, life at sea for prisoners still had significant disadvantages. Being below-decks, in a shared, never motionless common enclosure was almost overwhelming... a predicament the overworked ship's surgeon could do nothing to alleviate.

Privacy was always at a premium—particularly during rough weather while trying to balance on a bucket doing what comes naturally—exacerbated every prisoner's suffering.

Food however, though adequate, lacked variety and fresh water was rationed from day one, its quantity diminishing rapidly in step with its diminishing quality.

Two other matters raised their ugly heads to cause considerable torment: one physical, the other mental.

The prisoners were suffering badly in the many hours of their confinement. Being on or near the equator meant relentless, cloying heat. Even when free to be on deck to capture whatever breeze was created by the *Hougoumont's* passage, they all easily succumbed to sunburn, for shade was always scarce.

The second matter was an innate fear of the sea... a most unwelcome curse for some. By now, everyone on board had seen the huge grey forms that now escorted the *Hougoumont*. Only the most daring, or foolhardy, lingered long at the bulwark handrails when the wind picked up and the inevitable following swell caused the *Hougoumont* to pitch, or roll unpredictably.

* * *

During the period of equatorial passage, Brickie started to press his luck. He'd been warned of the consequences of misbehaving but persisted in irritating the free passengers with his derogatory comments, unwelcome hand gestures and sexually explicit innuendo. The prison guards initially turned a blind eye to these relatively minor infractions—some in fact being border-line humorous and attracted laughter, an always welcome pastime. But inevitably, Brickie's misguided sense of importance, his innate need for dominance and smouldering lust came to a head.

Two young girls, one in her mid-teens, were happily engaged in an innocent game of tag. As they ran along the starboard deck Brickie suddenly thrust out one of his legs tripping the pursuing teenager, sending her sprawling along the deck.

In an extremely quick pounce for such a large man, Brickie launched himself upon the hapless girl. In an even quicker series of movements one hand easily held the girl down, while the other was under her frock attempting to remove her under draws.

What Brickie had not previously noticed was Harry, sitting on an empty water keg not four yards away while quietly reading an old newspaper.

Harry had not seen the thug's initial tripping action, but looked up as soon as he heard the girl's shocked gasp as she clattered hard onto the deck. Harry jumped up, quickly appraising the girl's plight. In three fast determined steps, he delivered a vicious and well-placed kick into Brickie's exposed ribs.

Stepping back, Harry watched with satisfaction as the oaf roared in pain while rolling off and away from the distraught girl.

The girl, though shocked and already sporting a few bruises, scrambled away on her hands and knees into the protective arms of a nearby woman who had witnessed everything... so far. Though the woman tried to comfort the child, it was a difficult task as the teenager was shaking uncontrollably, whimpering and sniffling pathetically.

Gradually Brickie stood, holding his ribs and wincing in pain. 'Which one of you fuckin' bastards did that?' he bellowed and quickly followed that up with a nonsensical torrent of threatening abuse levelled at the gathering crowd.

'Me, though unlike you, I'll wager, I actually know both my parents,' Harry taunted in a strangely controlled voice. 'So what are you going to do about it? Bad enough that you hurt that poor girl, but to then attempt to molest and embarrass her in public... that's beyond any measure of decency.'

The last word had barely left Harry's lips when Brickie charged. There was no mistaking his rage; huge fists clenched tight as he ran, pig like eyes glaring, nostrils flaring and spittle dribbling from his mouth.

Brickie rapidly closed on Harry, but Harry was smarter and even quicker, his reflexes smooth and controlled. The thug attempted to deliver his first blow. But Harry side stepped, in the same motion grabbing Brickie by the collar of his shirt and the waistband of his trousers. With unexpected, surprising strength, Harry charged along the deck with his hapless, bewildered assailant doing everything possible not to over-balance.

Using the remarkable momentum that he'd built up, Harry suddenly released his struggling opponent, sending him flying head-long into the built-in section of the deck's aft bulwark—hoping that the impending blow would either stun him, or knock him out. But things quickly deteriorated. The stern's old woodwork smashed apart, no longer being capable of arresting Brickie's impetus.

As Brickie disappeared overboard and into the ship's wake, Harry realised immediately that the stupid oaf was in mortal danger. 'What have I done? The poor bastard can't swim, that's obvious, and despite that knock to his head he's also just realised *where* he is. Now the sod's petrified... and panicking. I can't just leave the dopey shit to drown. *I have to save him!*'

Without another thought, Harry kicked off his boots then started ripping off his clothes, but as he was about to throw his breeches to one side, he suddenly, surprisingly found himself restrained in a vice like bear-hug.

'Don't be stupid Harry,' demanded Patrick, his voice just loud enough for Harry to hear, but which he obviously did not immediately recognise. 'There's no saving him. Look. The *Hougoumont's* increasing her distance from him with every second. Even if you could get to him and hold his head out of the water, you'd never be able to swim back to the ship: you'd both then drown. Besides, there's no way the captain will attempt a recovery now.'

'Yeah, I suppose you're right,' Harry gasped in equal parts of acceptance and grief as he tried to shrug off Patrick's strong embrace. 'Nevertheless, that'll be a bloody cruel death. You do know he's absolutely shit-frightened of water... any water?'

In a calm but firm voice, Patrick said, 'Yes, I do know that, Harry. But mate, right now, that's the least of his worries. Look behind him; about twenty yards back.'

Unbeknown to the two observers, they couldn't see the blood oozing from the cuts inflicted to Brickie's head and neck. Regardless, it took Harry just a few heart beats to spot the three huge dorsal fins; all were closing on Brickie much quicker than the *Hougoumont* was increasing her distance from him.

Brickie's demise—from falling overboard to disappearing into the ocean's depths—was over in a less than two minutes.

Realising that he was no longer being restrained, Harry spun around to confront his temporary captor. 'Oh... it's you, Patrick. I didn't expect you to intervene. But thanks, anyway. Well, I suppose that's it then, I'm buggered, right? I'm gonna spend the rest of me bloody life in jail, that's for sure. You blokes will be looking for someone to blame for this.'

But before Patrick could speak, another authoritative voice replied, 'Not necessarily, son. Best you come with me and tell all. But first, please make yourself decent: get your breeches back on before you scare the wits out of most of these lovely ladies standing here. They are, after all, my best paying passengers.'

Despite the seriousness of the circumstances, the captain's good humour brought a ripple of laughter from the onlookers. 'And I want you to accompany us, Patrick; I'll need your account of what happened here.'

5

———

'Please be seated, gentlemen,' Captain Cozens instructed the two young men after they entered his cabin.

Addressing Harry, the Captain murmured, 'Right, Mr eh, eh?'

'Taylor; Harry Taylor, sir.'

'Ah, yes. I've read something about you. Please, Harry, do tell me everything that led up to this unfortunate event. Leave nothing out and do not exaggerate anything to suit your case.'

'There's not a lot to tell, sir,' replied Harry. 'But I'll do my best to explain my actions.'

The three men sat comfortably as Harry detailed his account. Ten minutes later, he abruptly finished speaking, gesturing with an open-armed flourish to reinforce the finality of his statement. 'Well, that's it, Captain Cozens.'

'Right. Now, Sergeant Galbraith, I need your account please.'

For the briefest moment, the significance of this formal address failed to register with Harry. But suddenly his eyes opened widely as if he'd been slapped; his mouth opened involuntarily and he spun to face Patrick. However, before an utterance could escape his mouth, Harry was forced into silence, first by Patrick's hand motion appealing to him to remain quiet, and secondly by Captain Cozens' intervention. 'Later Harry, hold your tongue for the present.'

A further ten minutes passed before Patrick, with aplomb, declared his account of events complete.

'For what it's worth, Captain Cozens,' Patrick continued boldly and earnestly, 'if England were at war, Harry would get decorated for the bravery I just witnessed. Look, given his current prisoner status, he's very aware how his actions in subduing Brickie could be used against him. So, Captain, I appeal to you on Harry's behalf that you look favourably upon his actions. After all, he single-handedly rescued that girl from be being brutally touched up. So fair go, Captain, please think how it'll weigh upon the poor bugger's good nature and his character if you recommend that he be punished.

'I agree,' said Captain Cozens in a tone of finality. 'My log will show that Brickie, or rather, Mr Bickford, was wholly and solely responsible for his own death. And Harry, your name will not appear anywhere in my report, other than that you were prevented by Sergeant Galbraith from committing certain suicide had you proceeded to dive into the ocean to save that man... or words to that effect. I'll see to it that neither of you hear anything further about this matter.

'I'll have you both know that I have details of Mr. Bickford's colourful, though particularly repugnant existence. How he's previously escaped the gallows I'll never know, but we're rid of him now.'

'Good riddance I say,' added Harry, 'though hopefully God will find a happier place for his soul.'

'That'll be all, gentlemen,' said Captain Cozens. 'Thank you both for your cooperation.'

As the two younger men exited the captain's cabin, they were greeted by a stiffening southwester and were forced to cover their eyes against the bright sunlight.

'I can tell by the look on your face, Harry, that we need to talk,' said Patrick with a conspiratorial smile. 'And so we shall. But first I'll have to let the guards know the outcome of that little meeting. How about we meet mid-ship in an hour? You've got my permission to be there if any of my men challenge you.'

Harry acknowledged Patrick's invitation with a nod and a brief wave. But just as he turned away, the almost forgotten teenage girl victim of Brickie's unwelcome attention ran to Harry, jumped onto his chest, simultaneously throwing her legs around his midriff and her arms around his neck... and hugged him tightly.

With equal urgency, she then released her arms, placed the palms of her hands onto either side of his face and stared into Harry's eyes. Before he could comprehend what was happening, the girl delivered the softest, warmest, and most sensual kiss the likes of which he had never experienced. 'Thank you, Harry. My name's Jane, and I'll be sixteen next year.' She then untwined herself, jumped back onto the deck and ran lithely towards her cabin; stopping once, to look over her shoulder and deliver the most playful, yet powerfully unambiguous sexual smile imaginable.

In somewhat of a daze and almost overwhelmed by the unfamiliar scent of early womanhood that now permeated his clothes and aroused his senses, Harry walked slowly back to his allocated space below decks.

6

———

Harry lay on his cot staring up at the construction of the deck's underside. 'Just how lucky *can I get*?' he cogitated. 'God only knows how it is that Jane has become a most unexpected *special* friend. And Patrick, he now seems to be my personal protector. Good God, I've only known *him* for five minutes.'

* * *

'AH, THERE YOU ARE, HARRY,' said Patrick, snatching Harry from his thoughts. 'Sorry I'm a bit late but the boys had more questions than I expected. Mind you, to a man they'll support you and they're all prepared to say they witnessed that bastard Brickie's dive overboard.'

'That puts me at ease; thanks,' Harry replied as he thrust out his hand. 'But don't you reckon it's high time we were formally introduced? That was quite a speech on my behalf. I'm grateful for sure, but why did you jump to my defence?'

'First, you did nothing wrong; you stood up to him. And second, well, because my father would not have been impressed otherwise.'

That said, Patrick sat on the deck beside Harry, relaxing in what shade covered their shared space. Companionable silence followed for a few minutes. They made an interesting sight; Patrick in his bright red Navy militia guard's uniform and shiny black boots, and Harry in his hand-me-down, now grubby white shirt, faded brown breeches and shoes approaching their used-by life. Both men were about six feet tall, broad-shouldered and well-muscled of solid build. Harry's hair was now bleached almost blonde, his eyes remarkably blue.

Both men were growing beards: Harry's through necessity for he had no means of shaving. Patrick's beard, which he wore by choice as a privilege of his military status, was jet black and as well-groomed as his equally dark hair.

Whereas Harry possessed a friendly (yet never to be underesti-mated) casualness, Patrick, perhaps because of his marine's back-ground, and perhaps because of his piercing dark brown eyes, had an unmistakable air of authority.

'So, I was right? Your father is none other than the Governor at Coldbath Fields Prison.'

'Correct, and I must say, you impressed him mightily, mate.'

'But why me?'

'It's quite simple, really. You reminded him of me. My father can be very firm in his job; he needs to be, having to deal with idiots like Brickie. But he also has a compassionate side.

'When I met with him during the week prior to this journey to bid him farewell, he mentioned of course that he'd read your convic-tion notes and was not only appalled by the ridiculous ruling handed down to you but was shocked to discover that he knew your father. In fact, surprise, surprise, our fathers had been friends for many years. I even recall him talking about your father when I was young.

'Initially they were early school chums, then went separate ways for a few years before catching up again. Our family were quite well off and saw to it that I joined the military, the Navy in fact. My parents bought me a commission and I became an officer, a junior lieutenant no less, specialising in procuring military goods and maintaining supply lines.

'Your father was a skilled carriage repairer and worked for my father. They also shared a long friendship until my father, considered as a gentleman, won a lucrative job at Coldbath Prison. It seems though, they drifted apart and never meet again.'

'Then it's possible I met your father way back then, but I can't recall ever doing so, or ever meeting you,' Harry replied thoughtfully.

'Yeah, likewise. Anyway, my father confessed to me that he was deeply saddened by your father's passing; more so that he had allowed their friendship to stagnate.

'He also believed he recognised elements of me in your demeanour—even when you were just a lad—so you must have met him. Apparently, when you came into his care at Coldbath he didn't immediately recognise you, but he certainly did after he'd read your conviction notes. He's told me all about you volunteering for transportation and how you went about it.

'The truth is, Harry, my father had great difficulty accepting your circumstances; circumstances which could so easily have befallen me. He was aware that I've nicked more things than you ever did and never got caught. He just wanted to see you right, as he hoped others might do if it had been me in your situation. I also reckon his intervention in lessening your distress at Coldbath was, well, his way of repaying his lost friendship with your dad.

'He also chose not to let you know of his past friendship with your dad for fear of being accused of prisoner favouritism: he could easily lose his job if found out. Instead, he charged me with the honour of passing on this news.'

'Well, I'll be buggered, but I truly am grateful. Mate, I just hope that my "good demeanour" keeps me out of trouble in the future,' Harry responded, 'but in the meantime it seems I'm collaborating with a bloody rogue!'

Both men smiled knowingly and then broke into laughter.

'By the way Harry, there's a few things you need to be aware of. First, whenever we're in earshot of anyone of either military rank or social status, it'll be best if you refer to me not by my name, but by my rank. In fact, there could be trouble for both of us if you don't.

'And second, now that we've left England and our circumstances have changed, we can drop that rot, unless it's to our advantage to do otherwise. You alright with that Harry?'

'Of course, you're calling the shots... lieutenant.'

'Incidentally Harry, have you ever wondered about that turnkey at Coldbath?'

'You mean, Hawkins? Not a bad sort after you get to know him.'

'Yes, that's the bloke. He's also a good friend of my father's and often takes care of matters for him. Does the thrashing handed-out to the gentleman who dobbed you in come to mind?'

'Yes, indeed it does. I had my suspicions, but I never did get to thank him for delivering that timely reward. Oh well, that's life, eh?'

'Hawkins also acted as my father's eyes and ears at Coldbath, not unlike my role for Captain Cozens here on board the *Hougoumont*. Of course, things'll change when we get to Fremantle.'

'Yeah, right; I'm back in the lockup and you're off gallivanting about, making yourself rich.'

'Not necessarily Harry, though getting rich does have great appeal.' Again, both men chuckled.

'Don't stress too much Harry. I've got a plan in mind that should, with a bit of luck, get you out of the lockup sooner rather than later.

'A word of advice though. I happened to see that beautiful young lady's advances. I'd forget her if I were you. Mind you, her mother is also a handsome lady; but too old for you, chum.'

* * *

DURING THE NEXT FEW HOURS, Harry and Patrick were to learn much more about each other and what had shaped their lives before their paths crossed on this voyage. There was no mistaking that a new, totally unexpected and trusting friendship had emerged between them.

It also surfaced that they shared common ambitions: both were driven to explore the world and perhaps to become one day, very rich. Both agreed that had they stayed in England, neither of those ambitions was foreseeably ever possible.

7

The *Hougoumont's* arrival at the Swan River Colony of Western Australia was greeted with a trickle of fanfare for the free travelling passengers. However, the hapless prisoners were quickly ushered from the dock and into their accommodations at the local Prison.

Conditions were an improvement on Coldbath Prison. The food was marginally better, the fresh water untainted, but always too little. Unexpected prison yard release gave the new prisoners the chance to breathe fresh air, to luxuriate in the sun's warmth and to experience the refreshing afternoon onshore sea breeze, which arrived with amazing regularity at the end of each hot day.

Though this prison was designed with a focus on prisoner reform, there was little respite for the inmates. All prisoners were subjected to ten hours per day of supervised work, however, there was no relief from the one thing that nagged at all of them and which they despised: their on-going loss of freedom.

* * *

'Prisoner Taylor,' a guard called loudly to where a group of a hundred or so men in the prison yard were having what was euphemistically referred to as their midday meal. Harry stood and was beckoned by the guard to join him.

'You've got a visitor, mate. Come along; you're wanted in the public meeting hall. You'll be on your own with your visitor, though I don't know how he got permission for that. Everyone else only gets visitors during the appointed times.'

Harry dutifully walked in front of the guard and was soon ushered into the meeting hall. 'Well, he's all yours now, Lieutenant,' the guard said, acknowledging the only other man in the hall, 'so I'll be on my way.'

Patrick walked briskly up to Harry, greeting him with a broad smile as he thrust out his hand. Their handshake was powerful, almost ferocious, a measure of the shared pleasure at this meeting.

'Great to see you again at last, Harry. You seem to be in reasonably good fettle, though I don't envy your stay here.'

'No one in their right mind would envy the pleasures of life in any prison, Patrick. On the other hand, you look like you've been eating roast duck while I've been eating feathers. Mind you, this place leaves Coldbath for dead.'

'Fear not Harry, you won't be returning to either place, I can guarantee you that. C'mon, let's sit here. I've got even better news: no, in fact, I've got great news!'

Intent upon giving his undivided attention, Harry turned to face Patrick full on, for he was now more than just a *little* excited to learn why his friend was so cheerful.

'It's amazing what a bit of authority and a freshly pressed lieutenant's uniform will do to cement a deal. Mind you, a letter confirming my excellent bona fides also had the desired impact, compliments of none other than Governor Galbraith's amazing foresight.'

'Also, something to do with your "impeccable demeanour" I dare say?' Harry jibed. 'But please... out with-it, Patrick, before I scream! Hang on! What did you just say about me *not returning to either place*?'

'That took a while for the penny to drop, eh, mate. But it's true... you're a free man; well almost.

'You see Harry, you've been *sort of officially released*: but you're now under my charge,' Patrick said proudly. 'In other words, I've arranged your Ticket of Leave... and here it is, mate.

'You can read it later,' Patrick added as he handed the very official looking document to Harry. 'In essence, this document allows a convict to work either for themselves or under the supervision of an authorised official... which of course, I am... provided you remain in a specific area, report regularly to local authorities and attend divine worship every Sunday. Normally however, you would not be permitted to leave this colony.

'But we got lucky, Harry. You see, the good Governor here succumbed to my Marine Lieutenant status and accepted my argument that if I take responsibility for your full-time supervision, then you can leave here, in my company, whenever I choose.

'What's more, while you're under my wing, there will be no need to report to other authorities until we reach Sydney Town. And between then and now, my friend, divine worship can go on hold, or be optional: that'll be up to you.'

The resulting looks on Harry's face were first of surprise, then incredulity, and finally, sheer unambiguous joy.

'But hang on, Harry. Stop fidgeting. I can tell you've got questions, but things get even better... so just sit tight for a moment or two longer and let me explain a few more things.

'It so happened that a few days after we landed at The Swan River Colony, another ship from England docked here with a cargo of about fifty live sheep. Being the curious lad that I am, I introduced myself to the ship's Captain who in turn introduced me to the proud but concerned owner of those sheep. It seems that three of the men he engaged to attend his animals have either proven to be unreliable or incompetent, or both. All of them claim that they are now too ill to continue and have effectively "disappeared."

'Regretfully the owner of the sheep no longer has enough workers to complete reprovisioning before the scheduled sailing date, or to properly attend his animals for the remaining part of his journey.

'Worse for the owner, the captain's made it clear that his priority is the making good of his ship ready to sail by the day after tomorrow. His paying passengers obviously have more say in things than those poor sheep.

'So without your consent Harry, but knowing how adventurous you are, and how adept you should now be in all matters relating to the handling and care of livestock—given your recently acquired knowledge while lounging around with Hawkins at Coldbath—I've signed you on to babysit those sheep. I'll chip in to help out; bugger my rank and privilege... more hands make the work lighter, eh?

'The pay won't be too flash and whatever you earn will be yours. I've seen the separate accommodations being offered to us and I must say they are a considerable improvement upon what we endured on the *Hougoumont*. I've also spoken with several of the paying travellers and without exception they claimed the food has been agreeable, though a bit monotonous. I reckon we could handle all of that well enough; what do you say?'

The look on Harry's face changed suddenly to one of possibly understanding where Patrick's plans were heading, but even so, he was in for a few more amazing surprises. Nevertheless, Harry suppressed his curiosity, leant back in his chair and gestured for Patrick to continue.

'As it so happens, Harry, I too spent some time on a farm when I was a just a lad. The servants who tended the sheep taught me just as much about them as they did about horses and dogs, so you won't be without my experience as trained help,' said Patrick as he ploughed on in his now familiar manner of understated humour and pragmatic good sense. 'We'll also get to see the colonies of Melbourne and Sydney Town when we dock for reprovisioning.

'Our destination sounds interesting; apparently, a place called Trial Bay. It's about three weeks sailing north of Sydney Town. The sheep are destined for their owner's property about forty or so miles inland, somewhere southwest of Trial Bay.

'But there's a catch to this proposition, Harry. You see, Trial Bay is also a prison site. The prison is still under construction; mostly convict labour, which is short on numbers and building skills. And regretfully, wait for it... part of the agreement I've struck with the Governor here at the Swan River Prison, is that we will both be put to work—for a period of not less than four months—assisting with the completion of that prison. Most irregular I know, but I'm not going to sit around and watch you do all the work; again, bugger rank and privilege.'

'But hang on, Harry,' said Patrick with a hands-up motion to refrain Harry from interrupting, 'there's a few sweeteners that should make this deal more palatable for us. First, your Ticket of Leave has been backdated to commence from the date of your arrest, not from the date of your sentencing.

'Second, your Ticket guarantees that all travelling time, including that while at sea moving between colonies, will be included in assessing the termination date of your sentence.

'Third, I've been assured that provided you keep your nose clean, don't cause any grief to other prisoners or the guards and don't abscond or try to abscond, then you can live in accommodation outside of the prison confines.

'Fourth, I was able to secure for you an additional "two for one deal," meaning that if you complete the four months' we've been assigned to at Trial Bay, you'll be credited time as if you had worked there for eight months. This means your record will then show that you will have served almost three of your original seven years' sentence.

'Or... but most significantly, at the expiration of our time at Trial Bay, we can petition the Governor at that prison to replace your Ticket of Leave with an Absolute Pardon... on the Governor's recommendation that you are a trustworthy soul, likely to make a good citizen.

'Mind you, you won't be allowed to return to England until your original seven years' sentence expires. I had to agree to this restriction, but I think we are of like mind on this condition. I, for certain, have no intention of ever returning to England.

'Well, what do you think Harry, a fair deal, or what?'

'You're absolutely right on that last point, Patrick,' replied Harry, his enthusiasm and spirit now soaring. 'Good God Almighty, mate. Of course I accept... anything beats seven more years in the nick. You've undoubtedly been very busy on my account again, and I confess that I'm in awe of your efforts. And again, I'm very bloody grateful, mate.'

'Well come on Harry, let's get you signed out and collect your belongings. You should still have some money in that canvas bag of yours if I'm not mistaken, so you can have the honour of shouting the first round of beer to celebrate your freedom. The local beer isn't too bad. But in all seriousness, Harry, whatever you do from this day on, *don't* lose or ever part company with that document you're holding!'

As the two men walked side-by-side away from the prison precinct, they alternated between animated jovial conversation, bois-terous laughter, and backslapping. Turning left onto the dockside, Harry playfully hip-bumped Patrick in the hope of catching him unawares and sending him flying. It succeeded, but there was no reprisal, just more good-natured laughter as Patrick stumbled and struggled to fall back into companionable step.

* * *

THE *SYLPHIDE* WAS a timber sailing-ship registered in Melbourne. It employed a rear mast, rigged fore-and-aft and two other forward masts, square rigged: a typical barque, except that its decks had been modified extensively to transport livestock as well as general freight. It was much smaller and had been in service for many years longer than the *Hougoumont.*

'Despite her vintage she's well maintained,' Captain Campbell said, at pain to assure Harry and Patrick of the seaworthiness of his ship, 'and she handles obediently and reliably in all weather condi-tions. You'll soon get accustomed to her.

'Just remember both of you, as I told Patrick yesterday, we *will* be departing Fremantle docks at high tide this evening: so, no "ifs or buts". I'm returning to Singapore via the Colonies of Melbourne, Sydney Town and of course, Trial Bay, where Mr Robert Eames—who you'll no doubt shortly meet—will take charge of offloading his precious sheep. But I'm on a tight schedule, so I need maximum effort from you two boys in loading that hay stacked alongside; and there are still twenty or so barrels of fresh water to be stowed. So please, get a move on. Yes, I know it's hot, but I see my second in command, old Mr Tilbury, has just returned with another load of hay and he's waiting patiently for you both to join him.

'Are you still happy to perform these deck duties, Patrick?' Captain Campbell asked quietly. 'You don't have to of course, but I'm in no mood to have you pull rank on me and stop work at the last minute.'

'I'd be offended if you really believe I'd do that. Just keep our arrangement to yourself and say nothing to any authorities... and we'll get on well, I'd say.'

'What about the sheep, Captain?' Harry asked. 'I mean, in this heat they must be feeling it. There's not much shade on offer, eh?'

'Why don't you ask Mr Eames about that while you're helping him load?' Captain Campbell replied curtly, his patience now wearing thin. 'Get a move on lads, times on the wing!'

'Aye, aye Captain,' Patrick called cheekily as he threw a mock salute, then spun around and raced down the central gangplank with Harry close on his heels. When on the dock, they sprinted over to the stack of hay where they introduced themselves to old Mr Tilbury (of unknown age) and the sheep's owner, Mr Eames, a man most likely in his mid-forties.

Hours of hard work followed without a break. The cracking pace which Harry and Patrick set resulted in all the hay and the last of the water barrels being secured below deck.

* * *

A MAGNIFICENT LATE evening sky preceded the sun sinking into the Indian Ocean as it farewelled another day. The tide was in full ebb as the lonely vessel slipped her berth. It then turned easily and slowly seaward, the usual onshore breeze having relented an hour earlier.

Harry had been conscientiously busying himself, when for no other reason than to have one last glimpse of the budding colony of Swan River, he casually gazed across the port side... and got the shock of his life.

There, standing alone on the dockside in the fast-fading daylight was a most captivating figure: Jane! It was not just her bewildering beauty, but her innocence, that caught his breath. Sheepishly, and feeling guilty, he waved. Enthusiastically, she immediately returned his gesture, then abruptly turned away.

Looking forlorn with her head lowered, Jane walked slowly from the dock into the gathering night. Had Harry been just a little closer, he would perhaps have heard her pitiful sobbing and seen the torrent of tears cascading down her cheeks.

                                    8
                          ____

H arry, Patrick, Mr Eames and old Mr Tilbury sat in a loose
     circle on the ship's deck, chatting amiably; all were tired
     but content. A gentle breeze refreshed the men but did
little to either ease their aching muscles or alleviate the multiple
weeping and itching scratches on their arms from manhandling
countless sheaves of hay.

Following a generous dinner of roast beef and vegetables, a bottle
of cool English beer was issued to each crew member, its contents
lasting only seconds.

'Bloody hell Patrick, that meal wasn't to be sneezed at, eh?', said
Harry while not bothering to disguise another loud belch. 'I haven't
eaten anything that nice for more than a year. But mate, how did
Captain Campbell's cook manage to get the beer so cold?'

'I can answer that,' Mr Eames replied casually. 'But before I do,
my name's Robert, so drop the *Mr* if you would please. Anyway, I
sincerely thank the both of you lads for what you've done to help
me out.

'Oh yes,' Robert continued after a brief pause, remembering
where he had meant to start his explanation. 'The colonials use an
ingenious storage box for cooling and prolonging the life of whatever

edibles they want to keep. For the box to work, they drape a wet cloth over it and keep the cloth wet. Apparently, it relies on what's called heat transfer; that's what happens as the water evaporates. The space inside the storage box magically becomes much cooler than the temperature outside. So long as the cloth's kept wet, our beer, for example, benefits rather nicely, as we've all just appreciated. They call it a Coolgardie safe, by the way.'

'I hope you've all made the best of it,' old Mr Tilbury interrupted, 'because unfortunately, Captain Campbell won't allow us any further grog until we get to Melbourne. After that he'll not give a rat's arse what you do, so long as you're all back on board before we depart for Sydney Town.'

'That was interesting stuff, Robert, and thanks for your tip off, Mr Tilbury,' replied Harry. 'But Robert, what about your sheep? They must surely be feeling this heat... with all that wool they're carrying and bugger all shade on deck?'

'I'm also concerned, Harry, but when I engaged Captain Campbell to transport my sheep, he assured me that this is the best time of the year for such an undertaking. He's sailed these waters five times so his experience and advice should prove invaluable.

'By the way, from my flock of forty-eight head, I've only lost two ewes since we left England, so I'd say there's a bit more than good luck involved. More importantly, there's no reason to believe his good judgment will be any different for the rest of our journey.

'Apparently, at this time of year, westerly winds dominate and according to Captain Campbell this means two very important things. If you think about it, our west to east passage means that solid shade from the sails will protect my sheep for most of each day. He also reckons our passage with a tail wind should be smoother and faster than at most other times.'

'That tail wind should also make life for all a bit more pleasant,' Patrick quietly interrupted, 'provided of course we don't hit a reef and sink.'

As the ensuing laughter abated, Patrick enquired politely, 'So Robert, tell us more about your sheep.'

'Well, they're called merino and they originated in Spain. They're a very important and popular breed of domestic sheep, not only in Spain but in England from where these beauties came. The merino is highly prized for its fine, soft, and lustrous wool and, because of their soft rolling skin, they're easy to shear and their pelts can be turned into rugs, winter jackets and even footwear. Plus, who can resist roast lamb, eh?'

'All of my ewes over there are quality animals, and I can assure you I paid big money for the four rams in the other pens. I can afford to lose a few more ewes, but not any of the rams; they're the cornerstone of my future success. They'll also see to it that all the ewes will be ready to drop their lambs by the time they get to my property.

'Therefore lads, please see to it that those boys receive your best attention. Mind you, I must accept that the final head count that'll complete this journey will still largely depend upon survival of the strongest.

'Large flocks of merino are already being bred in this amazing new country, and over time could make everyone involved in rearing them very rich. There's no reason why these sheep won't also thrive under the various climatic conditions and the terrain that exist on my humble holding near Trial Bay.'

'So you've been to New Holland previously, I take it?' Mr Tilbury asked quietly.

'Well, no,' replied Robert. 'As a matter of fact, I inherited the property from a relative I hardly knew. I really know very little about it other than a few brief words describing its surroundings and assets... oh, and I have a hand sketched map of its location, relative to Trial Bays position on the coast. Mind you, I have some experience working with sheep, so hopefully that'll see me right.'

Almost as an afterthought, Robert added, 'You boys will be most welcome to visit my property at any time. Now Patrick, perhaps you can tell us a little about you two?'

Patrick obliged, though his account was short on detail. Nothing was mentioned about Harry's modified prisoner status, or of the work he was expected to undertake at Trial Bay.

'It's fair to say that we both want to see and explore the world rather than settle down,' Harry added as a closing comment as he stood to leave, 'though that could change if the right women were to cross our paths. Good night, gentlemen.'

As Harry and Patrick were about to enter their respective sleeping quarters, Harry paused and said, 'Mate, I dunno about you but as tired as I am, I'm really looking forward to starting the next stage of this voyage. I hope Robert does well in his venture; he's not a bad chap, eh?'

'Yeah, agreed on all counts,' replied Patrick. 'Now, get some sleep because we're expected to be up before sparrow's fart.'

* * *

When Harry and Patrick were out of earshot, old Mr Tilbury yawned and said quietly to Robert, 'For landlubbers, not a bad couple of lads we've got there, eh?'

9

The ocean journey from Fremantle to the colony of Melbourne was as predicted. Apart from a few uncomfortable days during which the *Sylphide* developed an unnerving corkscrew motion as she charged eastward, the result of strong westerly winds and the Southern Ocean's persistent south westerly swells, near perfect sailing conditions and minimal discomfort for both man and beast otherwise prevailed. More importantly, there was no loss of life.

During this passage, teamwork bred camaraderie and new friendships flourished among the entire crew's company, in no small way due to Harry's youthful enthusiasm and Patrick's pragmatism.

'You've certainly grown your sea-legs, son; I'm impressed,' Captain Campbell remarked quietly to Harry after one particularly long stretch of night sailing. 'Most of those new to this caper usually suffer appallingly and quickly lose interest in their work... and then become a liability. But not so with you and Patrick.'

'Thank you Captain, but I reckon the trick is keeping busy; looking after these poor bloody sheep does it for me,' replied Harry. 'Besides, Robert's a brave and decent bloke and deserves some help.'

* * *

MELBOURNE BECKONED, but upon arriving in Port Philip Bay, they were greeted by the malodorous airs of concentrated humanity. Though the bay was crowded with many and all kinds of vessels from around the world, Captain Campbell expertly guided the *Sylphide* into what appeared to be the only available waterside berth.

Three days later, men and beasts refreshed and all necessary supplies replenished, the *Sylphide* was soon surging north, aided most favourably by a steady south-westerly wind.

All jobs now being reduced to watch-and-respond meant that Patrick had time to finally read the simple news bulletin he had collected on day one while in Melbourne.

'I say Harry, you must read this', said Patrick, as he handed over the newspaper while tapping his forefinger on the front-page head-line article.

A few minutes later, Harry replied as he handed back the newspaper. 'Seems to me those bushranger blokes are nasty bastards; to be avoided at all costs, I'd say.'

'Maybe so, young Harry, but how do you reckon you'd have survived if you had nothing... and no hope? Mind you, some of them do seem to be quite daring and enterprising chaps.'

10

'What do you reckon, Harry, Cape Town or Sydney Town? Which do you like most?'

'This takes the cake for me. Coming in here through those huge cliffs was a bit scary at first, but wow, this is one spectacular bay.'

'Agreed,' replied Patrick. 'Harbour, not *bay*.'

'Yeah, all right, but the stink here is probably worse than in Melbourne. Do you reckon people ever get used to it?'

'Regrettably the local fragrance *is* somewhat intense but try not to let it bother you too much. Trust me Harry, it won't be anything like this where we're heading.'

* * *

Amidst the hundreds of vessels at anchor within Sydney Harbour, Captain Campbell somehow uneventfully manoeuvred the *Sylphide* into what appeared to be the only remaining commercial berth. The small dock accommodated only four vessels, theirs being at the very end.

Their first week was spent locating, purchasing, and stowing provisions, not an easy task given the frenetic ebb and flow of dock-side humanity.

Towards the end of that period, it became evident that the vessel nearest to land was in a state of urgency to get under way. Accusations and threats were constantly being hurled at anyone who accidentally impeded their progress... particularly Captain Campbell's crew who had to bypass that vessel in their many errands.

Suddenly, during one of those confrontations, the unmistakable sound of a cracking whip crashed over the dock, immediately putting a stop to the general dockside hubbub.

Harry and Patrick looked at each other, dropped their loads and quickly pushed their way towards the sound, thinking that they might be needed to intervene to assist one or more of their crew-mates. What confronted them was soon clear. Workers had stopped work and formed an open space around a large, brutish individual who was ranting abuse, not at the dock workers... but at three defenceless, emaciated black people huddled together on the dock-side; their fear obvious, as were the bloody welts across their exposed arms and shoulders.

Harry and Patrick had previously seen these pitiful native folk; they had only been begging for food and had not been obstructing anyone.

The whip-wielding white man moved to better balance himself in readiness to again unfurl his blood-soaked whip... but his arm was forcibly stopped dead. He spun round to challenge whoever had the audacity to restrain him but was greeted with Harry's angry face and a very fast-moving fist about to smash into his face.

The man staggered back, his nose broken and bleeding profusely. Close to unconsciousness, he overbalanced, dropping the whip and landed flat on his back just inches from falling into the sea.

Harry stepped forward, dragged the man away from the dock's edge, picked up the whip, then ripped off the man's shirt... and stepped back.

'Now let's see how you like it, you miserable bastard,' said Harry as he looked into the man's bewildered eyes who was trying desperately to make sense of what had just befallen him.

The whip cracked viciously as it unfurled across the man's now naked back. He screamed in shock and pain. Too slow to fully gather his wits and move to avoid further punishment, a second savage stroke again drew blood and tore off another strip of bleeding white skin.

'That's enough, Harry!' Patrick demanded as he moved forward in an attempt to restrain his headstrong friend.

'No! No way, Patrick!' Harry protested, quickly moving away from his friend. 'Look! He's needlessly assaulted and hurt all those poor bloody blacks. And one's just a kid!'

'Right, he gets just one more, Harry. Make it a good one, then hand-over the whip to me before you kill him!' Patrick demanded.

'Know what it's like to beg, you bastard.' Harry yelled as he threw all his strength into his final whip stroke. 'That's it, bigshot, grovel and beg for mercy. I take it now that I've got your word you'll think twice before ever harming anyone again... regardless of their skin colour!'

'Alright you lot, this thug's got what he deserved,' Patrick yelled to the onlookers. 'Show's over, now get back to your jobs.'

* * *

'By the way, where'd you learn how to use a whip like that?' asked Patrick, as he walked with Harry back up the *Sylphides'* gangplank.

'Our old friend, Hawkins, remember him? When I was at Coldbath, your father ensured that Hawkins instructed me in the many and varied means of applying a whip. It takes one hell of a lot of practice to learn the art, but I had plenty of spare time on my hands to perfect it, if you remember.

'Yes, of course, but it's just as well you didn't kill that fellow,' Patrick replied matter-of-factually as he threw the offending whip into the sea, 'otherwise I'd have to arrest you. So, please Harry, pull your head in just a bit, eh?'

11

———————

Three days later, the *Sylphide* had made first-rate progress northwards: sheets full, ropes rigid and singing, boards and masts creaking and trailing a continuous pearl-white wake for several hundreds of yards.

During a lull in deck activities, Robert asked his group of friends who sat in relaxed good company around him, 'So what became of those poor bloody black folk? I never saw them again after that little distraction on the dock back there.'

Captain Campbell was quick to reply. 'Sad news I'm afraid. The two oldest, parents of the young boy, I think, are both dead. Bled to death I was told.'

Disbelief and disappointment struck not just at Harry's heart, but at the hearts of all those who had witnessed the dockside flogging that those old folk had endured.

'And the boy... what became of him pray tell?' Harry asked quietly, seething inwardly at the possible implications.

'Why not ask him?' the captain replied as he gestured towards his cabin, 'he's standing over there behind you lot, though I suggest he's out of earshot.'

'And what did you learn about that thug?' Harry muttered.

'As a matter of fact, the skipper of his vessel sacked him, without pay and the crew gave him one hell of a going away party,' Captain Campbell explained. 'It wouldn't surprise me though, that if the flogging you gave him didn't kill him, then the handshakes and back slapping of endearment from the crew as he tried to leave, probably did. Mind you, no one seemed to know what became of his body.'

'Good riddance, I'd say,' Patrick replied with finality as he walked over to the black youth, determined to let him know that not all white men were cruel bastards.

* * *

UNSCHEDULED STOPOVERS, first at Newcastle and then at Port Macquarie, were necessary when the weather deteriorated rapidly. On both occasions their luck held, and they made safe and protected moorings before the seas turned perilously wild. And on both occasions, though they dodged the worst of the strong winds, they did not escape the accompanying torrential rain.

Two other northbound vessels which had recently overtaken the *Sylphide* were not at anchor when they arrived in Port Macquarie, their fate unknown.

But every cloud has a silver lining. Rain soon filled their water storage barrels, and there was joy for the entire crew knowing that there was ample fresh water to wash the saltwater from their clothes, hair and malodourous bodies.

With equal good luck at each subsequent unscheduled stopover, the winds had abated within a few days; Newcastle being no exception.

After three more weeks of steady, uneventful sailing, Harry, Patrick and Robert, all so tantalisingly close to starting their new lives, were becoming increasingly impatient to be rid of the *Sylphide* and to set foot at their destination.

Captain Campbell, resolute in safely reaching his own far distant objective of Singapore, understood their frustration and finally announced that by his reckoning, they could reach Trial Bay within the next twenty-four hours.

And so they did. Midday the next day, after rounding a small headland, there on the crest of the small hill that swept almost continuously around the bay, stood an unfinished blockwork structure; undoubtedly, Trial Bay Prison. A few rudimentary stone and timber huts could also be seen scattered along the ocean-facing sand-hill.

In addition to the prison they quickly spotted a stone structure jutting into the bay, obviously an uncompleted breakwater.

'I say, Robert, have you got any idea how many man-hours have been spent so far in building the prison and constructing the break-water?' Patrick asked.

'No idea really, but heaps, I'd say.'

'Regardless,' Patrick replied, 'we can all be grateful the break-water will provide a reasonably safe anchorage and some protection from the waves as they curl around that headland... provided this onshore breeze doesn't pick up.'

As soon as both forward and aft anchors were set, a dinghy was launched to transport Captain Campbell, Robert and Patrick ashore. They were eagerly met by three men.

Still puffing from their descent to the beach, the oldest and most official-looking man greeted each of the three arrivals with a firm handshake and an affable smile.

'Gordon O'Rourke's the name and welcome to Trial Bay. I'm the settlement and project administrator here for the Trial Bay Jail Authority and these two chaps are my most trusted assistants, Jim and Alf.

'So all up, how many folks do I have to accommodate? And have you brought the food and equipment I ordered?'

'Only three men will be disembarking,' replied Captain Camp-bell, 'these two gentlemen and one other, a prisoner; all genuine and reliable individuals you'll soon learn.

'Mr Galbraith here, or rather, Lieutenant Galbraith, has a pris-oner, Mr Harry Taylor under his direct supervision. Oh, I nearly forgot, there is also a young aboriginal boy on board, an orphan; quiet, but a good kid and he may want to come ashore. In fact, he can't stay onboard the *Sylphide*, my next port is in Singapore.

'The rest of my crew will stay on board to mend our mooring as necessary and to alert me in case of any mischief. They'll also be at your disposal to assist as required when we start off-loading your supplies.

'As for your supplies, here's your manifest, Gordon; all accounted for at loading. Mostly grain and food sacks, but several medium sized crates and smaller boxes, six small fruit trees, several other loose items such as masonry hand tools, shovels and agricultural items like axes and... and well, that's it... except for forty-six Marino ewes and four rams.'

'Good, good; you've done well. In fact, you've saved the day, our food and general chattels have been getting quite low. Thank you, Captain Campbell,' Gordon replied. 'And I can assure you all there will be no mischief afoot, as you put it. My internees know the consequences of any misbehaviour.

'If you wish, I can easily accommodate the four of you gentlemen overnight, and I can also assure you that it will need to be a real team effort to off load everything before night-fall. The sheep could become a problem if the wind picks up. But don't worry needlessly, Jim and Alf have done this before so I'd suggest we get a move on with Robert's sheep.

'By the way, you don't need to worry about that black lad, Captain, he was seen swimming for our breakwater, about twenty minutes ago. I'm sure he'll be long gone by now; I just hope he can look after himself. I fear he'll be as much in a foreign country, as say, a Frenchman in Romania. And, probably, no language in common with the locals.'

True to form, Jim, Alf and Robert soon had the sheep being slung two at a time into each of four dinghies as soon as they positioned themselves alongside the *Sylphide*. Thankfully, blindfolds calmed the ewes, though there were a few anxious moments when it was time for the rams to go ashore. Luckily, none of the dinghies capsized.

By the time all the sheep were ashore, a small crowd had gathered. Jim and Alf quickly organised the bystanders to usher the sheep up the sandy track to the settlement on top of the hill. Robert then took control of proceedings to keep his flock together and with his enthusiastic helpers, shepherded the sheep into a crude holding yard made from interwoven tree branches.

Off-loading the settlement's supplies was tedious and hard work, which continued into the twilight.

Trial Bay's new guests—and the unexpected helpers; all convicts as it soon transpired—were then all treated to a very welcome, but basic meal washed down with mugs of beer donated by the good Captain Campbell.

A quiet word from Gordon soon after resulted in the helper's bidding goodnight to their guests before heading in an orderly fashion back to their tents. It was very evident to Harry and Patrick that there was something unusual about this place; not what they were expecting.

* * *

HARRY WAS early awake the next morning, despite his aching limbs. The accommodation he shared with Patrick was basic; a two-man tent supplied with off-the-ground beds. Each bed had interlaced rope bases, a thin kapok mattress, two blankets and something resembling a pillow. Best of all though, blissfully gone was the rolling and pitching of his bed in concert with an ever-restless ocean.

Unbeknown to Harry, Patrick had already risen and vacated the tent.

Harry poked his head outside, but because there was no sign of Patrick, he quickly dressed, exited the tent and walked to the top of the hill that surrounded the bay. There, he took three deep breaths savouring the cool, ozone laden sea air.

Sudden movement on the beach below caught his attention and he soon realised it was Patrick, Gordon, Jim, Alf and Robert, all waving their farewells to the *Sylphide* as she pivoted on the early morning offshore breeze and nosed her way elegantly towards the open ocean.

Disappointed that he had failed to offer his personal thanks to Captain Campbell, Harry sighed, then sat on the hilltop and watched as the *Sylphide* gathered speed. Only after the trader had disappeared into the misty north did he look about.

The sun had risen over the Pacific and bathed the sand dunes and coastal scrub with a golden glow. In contrast to the deep blue of the ocean, each small wave was brilliant white where it curled and collapsed before flooding the beach, leaving sheets of sparkling foam on the sand as the water retreated.

Both north and south, a light mist draped itself lightly over the foreshore.

He then stood and turned to gaze into the distant hinterland. His vision quickly locked onto the blue-grey mountain range that had accompanied Patrick and him all the way from Melbourne... and now continued, weaving its way northward as far as he could see.

Next, he scanned the small settlement. Most dwellings had wooden frames, stone walls and bark rooftops. All had at least one door, glazed windows and stone chimneys, and doubtless, more home comforts than their tent offered. Furthermore, Harry noticed that every dwelling was cleverly aligned to catch any sea breeze that might rise from the bay.

Off to his left, there were also two rows of twelve white tents: temporary construction worker accommodation. Two hundred yards beyond them were at least sixteen white crosses.

Harry then sat on a nearby log and surveyed the new, partially built jail. Despite what this building represented, this was an important moment in his life, reminding himself of his remarkable good fortune in so many ways... his unexpected mate-ship with Patrick, his previous incarcerations almost forgotten, having avoided two possible murder charges, his good health and growing strength, the looming excitement of a new life and the potential adventures that lay ahead.

Though technically still a prisoner, he actually now felt very much as if he was totally free!

Not for ten months had Harry thought about his mother, but now admitted to himself that, although he had always loved her dearly, he was glad the shackles of his previous responsibility for her safety no longer emotionally burdened him. Nevertheless, he yearned her praise to some degree and secretly believed she would forever be proud of him.

In this moment of euphoria, the sound and songs of at least eight different birds and twenty different insects and the balmy, luxurious early morning breeze intruded upon his thoughts.

Not surprisingly, Harry jumped defensively when he suddenly felt a hand rest on his shoulder. 'Beats Coldbath Fields, eh, Harry?' Patrick said quietly as he sat on the log alongside his friend.

'That's for certain, mate. This place is an absolute paradise... prisoner or not.'

12

'Didn't want to wake you Harry, obviously you needed a good sleep judging by your shameless snoring. Be that as it is, I have to say you made an excellent impression upon Captain Campbell. He sends you his best wishes for the future and asked me to tell you that should you ever wish to join his trading company, there will always be a job for you. And me too, it seems.

'C'mon, let's get some breakfast. Gordon wants to give us the grand tour and acquaint us with the rules.'

* * *

'RIGHTO LADS,' said Gordon with authority. 'Listen carefully because I am not in the habit of explaining things more than once. Please accept whatever I say, or request, because it *is* the gospel here.

'My tenure expires in eighteen months. So by that time I want this jail completed and fully functional. And as you two have no doubt observed, we are making reasonable progress. Nevertheless, months of dedicated work remain ahead of us.

'As you have now seen, there are five men already imprisoned. They are all very nasty bastards; stand-over merchants, murderers and rapists. They each get two hours out of their cells every day during which time they will be shackled hand and foot. You are not to fraternize with them! Do I make myself clear? These are non-repentant, bad individuals!

'However, it may surprise you that they are all scheduled to be released in about two years' time; provided of course that I don't find some good reason to have them all hanged in the interim.

'By contrast, you have otherwise no doubt noticed that we have an easy-going order here and that there is a high degree of cooperation. I have great sympathy for them all; most are here for transgressions no greater than stealing three potatoes, or for borrowing things without first seeking permission... just to keep their wife and kids fed.

'Look, I know it's most uncommon, but we operate here with enlightened attitudes; mostly mine. These people are neither animals nor savages. Nor are they stupid yokels. There will be no excuse for whippings or other harsh treatment of these people while I'm in charge.

'To a man, my judgement says they are all good men, trustworthy and grossly unfortunate to be in their respective predicaments. I therefore have no objection should you wish to mingle with and hopefully befriend these men.

'In fact, it's important that you do get on well with them, because Harry, some of these men are experienced and master stonemasons who will become not only your teachers, but your on-the-job bosses whose word is final. Should you cause any disharmony or instigate fights, you'll be in lockdown so fast you won't have time to fart.

'What also makes this cooperative concept work is that all these men receive payment as a monthly stipend that only I can authorise. Upon their release, they can convert it into legal tender. It's not much, but they will not end up penniless, so it helps to keep them focused and out of trouble. They misbehave; their stipend is cancelled for the next two months.

'Three more matters. You've no doubt seen all ten women during our grand tour. All have husbands living with them here, so they must be respected and acknowledged, because they'll be preparing most of your meals and will, for a small payment, wash your clothes if you ask politely.

'Work clothes and footwear will be issued to you later today, Harry. The headwear you'll receive may not be fashionable but don't underestimate its importance. Three of those poor souls in our cemetery are testimony to the sun's strength and don't be fooled by the sea breeze either, it won't save you from the sun's rays.

'Well Harry, you start work after breakfast tomorrow. You'll be introduced to your workmates then; you'd be wise to reflect on my advice. Remember, if you have problems, you talk to me first.'

'Any questions?'

'Not questions,' Patrick replied, 'but rather, I want my position here understood, Gordon. I'm here as a serving Royal Marine Officer which gives me implied responsibility to maintain order. I also have legal guardianship of Harry Taylor until the termination of his Ticket of Leave.

'It's not my intention to usurp your authority here, Gordon, in fact, I look forward to working with you, when and if required. But any discipline or punishment imposed upon Harry will be entirely at *my* discretion; including when I decide to leave this settlement. Rest assured however, that Harry *will* complete his time here and that he understands his obligations.

'I also intend to collaborate with your men in whatever capacity. So have you got enough work clothes and boots for one more?'

'Thanks Patrick, I understand: a bit unconventional, but yes, any assistance you can provide is most welcome. So go along with Harry tomorrow and get kitted out.'

'Just two questions,' Harry asked quietly. 'Are you aware, Gordon, that we came to this country on one of the last prisoner transport ships to ever leave England? So how many new prisoners do you now expect will continue to arrive here to serve-out their time?'

'No, I didn't know that Harry,' replied Gordon, sounding a little affronted. 'The powers-that-be have not yet conveyed that long overdue situation to me, formally or otherwise. Mind you, in theory we should see fewer long-term prisoners at Trial Bay, but regrettably, the fact is there will never be a shortage of criminals running free in this country.'

'Before we take our leave Gordon,' Patrick continued. 'I noticed old horse droppings in the sheep enclosure. 'Where are the horses now, may I ask?'

'Long gone I'm afraid, Patrick. Person's unknown obviously believed they needed them more than I did... the bastards! Bushrangers no doubt and not a sign of them or my horses since.

'Both of them are bay geldings and good types, though they did have a bit of age on 'em. I'd know them anywhere; they've both got a small white blaze on their foreheads and whitish tufts of hair just above their hooves. Anyway, I've still got the saddles and bridles which will come in handy one day soon, I hope.'

'Your horses would have been especially useful for mustering and driving Robert's sheep to wherever he's going,' Harry suggested matter-of-factly. 'So how does he intend to move his sheep; he can't possibly do it alone. And when, pray tell, does he intend to take his leave? Do you know?'

'I discussed this with Robert yesterday,' Gordon replied. 'He's got his mind set on departing the day after tomorrow.

'Jim and Alf have volunteered to walk with Robert for four or five days, then return here. They'll both be issued with rifles and some ammunition... just in case they run into any trouble. I've also seen to it that all three men will be issued with basic food items, which they'll somehow have to carry of course.

'I hold no fears for Jim and Alf, but God only knows how Robert will cope after they part company.'

13

Patrick and Harry threw themselves into life at Trial Bay. They were also unexpectedly allocated idyllic sites upon which to build their own cottages. So welcome were they both made that the prisoners of Trial Bay assisted their new guests to locate and haul local rock and suitable framing timber to those sites. Experienced stonemasons then worked with Patrick and Harry to produce hand sketches to guide them with the construction work ahead.

* * *

Two weeks after the departure of Jim and Alf, Gordon was naturally becoming increasingly concerned: had his most trusted inmates absconded, fallen victim to a felon or felons unknown... or had the poor buggers starved? he wondered.

But Gordon need not to have worried, for late in the afternoon of that same day, two familiar riders unexpectedly arrived at the settlement... Jim and Alf!

'Well I be damned,' Gordon said excitedly to Patrick, 'they've not only found my horses, but look, they've got two strangers in tow, and all trusted up like turkeys, eh? I can only wonder what they've been up to.'

'And if I'm not mistaken, that's the young Aboriginal kid who sailed with us from Sydney Town,' Patrick replied.

After welcoming Jim and Alf, Gordon and Patrick escorted the two very disgruntled men to their own separate, recently completed jail cells.

* * *

'Well come on you two, out with it,' Gordon demanded as soon as Jim and Alf had devoured their specially prepared meals. 'Start with Robert Eames, please.'

'No need to concern yourself, Guv,' said Jim, 'he was like, confident that he'd soon arrive at his property; he had a map. He was safe and real healthy like when we turned for home.'

Alf quickly added, 'We watched 'im 'til he disappeared. His sheep were all still taggin' along behind 'im.

'And, oh yeah, he wanted us to pass on his thanks to you, Guv... most definite he was.'

'Thanks to both of you; well done,' replied Gordon. 'But come on lads, how on earth did you find my horses and capture those two ruffians... and pray tell, why did you bring the black kid back with you?'

'We'd best start with the black kid, Guv... if you don't mind,' Jim interrupted. 'As best as we can understand him, his name is *Eye Lewky*, but he responds to *Lukey*, or *Luke*, so we're going to call him Luke from now on. His English isn't too bad if yah listen closely.

'Anyway, we came upon a mob of natives not long before we farewelled Robert. Luke confidently greeted us with four adults, not threatening like, and as best as we could understand they were thanking us for returning Luke. He was born in this area—his tribal land, he reckons.'

'Now, that's a job for Harry and Patrick to further investigate,' said

Gordon with authority and impatience. 'We'll talk further about that later. Press on lads if you would.'

'Luke stayed with us and it was just as well he did,' Alf chimed in, 'because the very next day two geezers rode up and demanded money from us, believin' we'd just been paid for shepherding Robert's sheep. These same men had shot at Luke's mob the day before. Come to think of it, we thought we'd heard gunfire, but we didn't pay much attention because we didn't think it was coming from where Robert was heading.'

'Yeah, but they came a gutzer,' Jim added quickly, 'the silly buggers were full as googs and didn't seem to notice that me and Alf already had our rifles pointed straight at 'em, like. But when Luke made a fuss; pointing time after time at the tree line where a dozen or more of his heavily armed mob were standing not thirty yards away, those gentlemen got most jittery and took off, real sudden like.

'Anyway, that's when me and Alf recogonised the Guv's horses.'

'And... then what?' Harry asked impatiently.

'Well, that evening,' Jim continued matter-of-factly, 'Luke took off after he'd eaten dinner with us. But he surprised the *bejabbers* out of us when he returned as the moon was setting, riding on one horse, and leading the other one... both saddled and with bridles and saddle bags.

'Luke had even collected all their rifles and handguns and their ammo; how about that, eh?

'The laddie had just slipped into the gentlemen's camp where they were both snoring their heads off. To make his point, like, he then produced three near empty bottles of rum from a saddle bag, which he explained had been lying beside the sleeping men.'

'Anyway, regardless that it was now quite dark, Luke easily led us back to the thieves' camp where Jim and me soon had 'em well tied up, like.

'The rest was easy. The next morning we tied their own ropes around 'em and connected 'em one to each saddle. As we rode the horses forward, they was forced to follow; bad luck for them how crook they were both feelin'. Anyway, that's about it. So, it's now over to you, Guv. What do you reckon you'll do with 'em?'

'They'll remain in prison here until a circuit magistrate arrives to decide their fate,' Gordon replied. 'Extremely well done, all three of you. Your actions will be recorded and I'll strongly advocate a reduction in your sentences as your reward.

'And of course, that will include a note of appreciation to Luke and his mob.'

'We'll now take a break and resume back here in an hour's time.'

* * *

FLUSTERED, Gordon strode back into the room. 'Where in God's name is that Black kid? I mean, Luke!

'He was supposed to be in your care Harry, but one of the ladies just told me they saw him walking away with a much older Black man... his father, I hope.

'Mind you, I suppose the lad should be safe enough with his kind.'

'No Gordon, not his father... *her husband!*' Harry replied with a broad mischievous smile on his face while trying not to burst out laughing.

'You see Gordon, our Luke is most definitely *not* a boy; her name is *Yarran*, and she *will* be perfectly safe in his care.'

* * *

REGRETTABLY, there was no way either Harry or Patrick would ever learn that another of Yarran's future actions of decency and compassion would unwittingly put their lives at risk.

14

A year seemed to pass in a flash, by which time not only was the Trial Bay jail close to completion, but so too were Patrick's and Harry's cottages.

'I've been thinking,' said Patrick to Harry as they sat in their favourite place overlooking the bay. 'There are many more free families living here than this time last year, and even if the jail was one hundred percent complete, it's currently housing less than a third of its capacity.'

'Yeah, so what's on your mind Patrick?'

'That it's time to move on. For me, anyway. I suppose that I'm ambitious, Harry, but not in the normal sense of settling down with a job or owning a farm: it's more like I'm somehow driven by a need to travel and see the world while I still can.'

'Mate, you must be a bloody mind reader. I was toying with exactly that, only last week.' Harry paused for half a minute before continuing. 'I agree and feel the same. So, if you don't mind that I tag along with you, when do you want to leave... and in which direction?'

'You're more than welcome of course; besides I'd be mad to do any such journey alone. South would be my first choice, but to where exactly, God only knows.

'I think it only fair that we let Gordon know our intentions first, but I also think it would be the decent thing to give him another two weeks of our time, at least now that the general focus is upon completing the breakwater; it's just about finished, eh?

'During that time, it should be possible to sell our cottages at a reasonable price and that'll give us a few quid to make an offer to buy Gordon's horses. As you know, for some reason he's now got four of them and hardly ever rides them, so he just might agree to sell three of 'em to us. We're going to need a good pack animal to carry most of our belongings.

'However, Harry, there may be a stumbling block to our plans. Hang on, hang on,' Patrick said before Harry could protest. 'Keep your shirt on. Let me explain.

'Do you remember our good fortune at Swan River jail where the governor put certain conditions on your future custody under my care? Well, I'm certain you've met all those conditions, but regardless, I'll now petition Gordon to replace your Ticket of Leave with an Absolute Pardon... on his formal recommendation that you are a trustworthy soul, likely to make a good citizen, of course. Which will mean when we leave here, you *will* be totally free. So I hope you haven't done anything that I don't know about... to put Gordon offside, I mean?'

'No bloody way, he's more like my father and he's a good friend. And as I've said before, I've no intention of ever returning to any jail, or to England for that matter.'

* * *

It really wasn't a surprise to Patrick that Gordon agreed with all his submissions on Harry's behalf. But it was a surprise when Gordon produced a formal decree from the circuit magistrate who had earlier visited Trial Bay... the document which already granted Harry his absolute freedom.

Gordon further surprised Patrick and Harry by not only gifting to them the three horses they asked for, but also by announcing he had several new residents very interested in purchasing both of their cottages.

* * *

AT DAWN, two weeks later, Harry and Patrick quietly rode away from Trial Bay with their pack horse in tow. Though neither of them talked for some time, both men were genuinely saddened at leaving behind so many unexpected and good friends.

The previous evening, they had shaken hands for the last time with all those people at a small gathering held on the crest of the hill overlooking the bay. Though their parting conversations were genial and sincere, nevertheless there was an air of mystery surrounding their destination, not because they refused to say, but because they really had no idea where that might be.

'Maybe Melbourne one day,' Harry was heard to say on a few occasions, whereas Patrick just shrugged his shoulders and shook his head and replied philosophically, 'Honestly, we'll just be taking things as they come.'

* * *

THREE DAYS LATER, following Alf's and Jim's instructions, Harry and Patrick arrived at Robert Eames' sheep station located near the small settlement of Frederickton.

'Do you reckon we've got the right place?' asked Harry, as he scratched his head. 'there's not a sign of him. Can't see any sheep and the roof of that cottage has collapsed completely.'

'Yeah, and the fences are totally buggered,' replied Patrick, clearly disappointed. 'That's not like the Robert we knew. He'd never let things get out of control like this. Well come on, we've got little option; let's keeping moving.'

As they were leaving the abandoned property, a lone rider approached. 'Can I help you?' he asked, his tone somewhat aggressive yet cautious.

'Maybe,' said Harry. 'We were hoping to find our friend Mr Eames living here, but there's no sign of him.'

'That's right, he walked away from his property after just a month or so. Sold this property and his few sheep to me for a bargain price I couldn't refuse, so he wasn't penniless. Dunno all his personal ins and outs for movin'. He seemed like a nice chap, but he was understandably dejected.'

'Ehm,' Patrick sighed. 'Well that's a blow, we were really looking forward to meeting him again. You wouldn't have any idea where he went, I suppose?'

'Nah, not really,' the local horseman replied. 'He could be dead for all I know. Nevertheless, there was a rumour goin' around here that he was seen in Gloucester; that's a good eight day's riding from here. I can give you some general directions if you're headin' that way.

'And by the way, you'll need to keep your wits about yourselves and keep your firearms close to hand, because if you're intent on goin' to Gloucester, you need to know there's still a few bushrangin' bastards likely to be plying their trade along the way.'

'Thanks and much appreciated', Patrick replied. 'We'll take you up on your directions, but really we've got nothing they'll want, eh Harry?'

'Those gentlemen got names?' asked Harry.

'Yeah, of course, but I haven't crossed paths with any of 'em,' replied the local. 'I don't know any of 'em by sight, but no doubt you'll hear about 'em soon enough… a chap known as Captain Thunderbolt for instance. Mind you, no one's seen or heard about him for some time. Cops might 'ave nailed him, but we wouldn't necessarily hear about it for months.'

15

A short distance south from Frederickton, Patrick and Harry rode into Kempsey, their intention being to top up their supplies.

However, as they dismounted at the general store conveniently located next door to a small pub, two young boys, one white, the other Black and both about fourteen years old, strolled past side by side. They were obviously enjoying each other's company, laughing perhaps at a new joke.

Outside the pub were five local men and judging by the number of empty glasses sitting on the pub's front windowsill and their loud, bawdy conversations, all were in an advanced stage of inebriation despite the early time of day.

Patrick and Harry ignored them, until one of the drunks threw his near empty glass at the boys and then ran, swearing unintelligible abuse, straight toward them. In his last stride, the drunk king-hit the unsuspecting Black youth, knocking him backwards onto the road, unconscious, his nose bleeding profusely.

The drunk looked back at his mates, a stupid smile on his face and raised his arms in the air as if he now deserved their hero-worship.

But as he was about to return his attention to the Black lad, readying himself to no doubt deliver a fearsome kick into the boy's midriff, he suddenly found himself being yanked backwards with great force and about to land most awkwardly on his arse right in front of his friends.

Bewildered and feeling the effects of his alcohol consumption the drunk staggered to his feet. But as he raised his head to orient himself, the last things he saw for the next several minutes was the furious expression on Harry's face and the huge fist about to slam into his face.

Broken teeth, blood and spittle were sent flying before the drunk once again landed heavily flat on his back on the road; he too, now unconscious and bleeding profusely from a badly disfigured nose.

Emboldened by the grog, the drunk's mates shambled onto the road, no doubt intent upon avenging their mate.

Booom... a shotgun roared, delivering its load of lethal pellets onto the road in front of the would-be rescuers. Instinctively they all ducked, but too slow to avoid a shower of stinging pellets, mud and road gravel.

Taking advantage of the stunned men's totally dissipated feelings of heroics, Patrick broke open the breech of the shotgun and then draped it casually into the crook of his arm. 'I'd stop whatever you had in mind, boys. You really don't want to upset my friend over there again; he's likely to get even more angry with you lot for not stopping that idiot, your so-called mate, for what he just did to that defenceless Black kid. So go and sit down and keep quiet, or better, piss-off, the lot of you!'

Meanwhile, Harry was helping the very nauseous and unsteady drunk to his feet. 'Here, put your hand out and take these. If you're wondering what I've got for you... well it's the last of your stinking, rotten teeth. You should hang on to 'em as a keepsake to remind you what you just did.

'And, hey! Are you idiots over there listening carefully? Good. Try to imagine what I'll do to you next time if I ever learn of a repeat performance. Now, go on, get lost!', Harry added as he gave the hapless drunk one last kick to his backside, sending him stumbling after his now retreating, almost sober cohorts.

Harry rubbed his knuckles, made a fist, flexed his fingers, then walked across the road and stood beside Patrick. 'No damage done. However, how the hell did you get your hands on that shotgun? I must say, a most timely intervention, nevertheless.'

'See that chestnut horse outside the pub and the empty gun case beside the saddle? Well, the horse and the missing gun belong to a local cop who, as you can now see, has just returned to the real world after his most recent dalliance with one of the barmaids. Anyway, I borrowed his gun when it looked like you'd need my help.'

'You what?'

'Yeah, I borrowed his shotgun and just as well he'd left one up the spout, eh?

'Can't stop to chat for the moment Harry, I'd better return it I suppose. I'll explain to him it accidently discharged somehow and if he wants to argue the toss, I'll accompany him to the police station where he can explain to his sergeant his reason for being otherwise detained while supposedly enforcing the law and keeping the peace.'

'Right, that should just about do it though I'd play it low key and very polite like, if I were you, Patrick.'

'All should turn out alright. I'm positive my Naval ranking carries more weight than that of any regional police sergeant.'

* * *

NOW FULLY PROVISIONED, Harry and Patrick again turned their mounts southward.

'I hope the Black lad gets some medical attention, but he'll probably need more help than he'll find here,' Patrick said with genuine compassion. 'I suspect he's going to be upset for some time, poor little bugger.'

'If it's any consolation,' Harry replied quietly, 'When you were tallying up, the white kid came back to thank us for "squaring up" as he put it. That was after he'd taken his mate to the only doctor in the town. A good boy, that.'

16

From Kempsey, the tracks to Gloucester were in a reasonable state of repair, though in places quite steep. For several days the weather was windless, warm and humid and took its toll on man and beast. This made it necessary for the men to take prolonged rest and for them to dismount and walk, particularly uphill, so as not to punish their aging horses.

'Hey Patrick, have a look at the massive canopies on some of these trees. I wonder how the undergrowth has grown so thick; surely not enough sunlight reaches the ground to support such dense growth?'

'Yeah, those trees are huge alright and they sort of provide a road tunnel. Just listen to all those different bird calls, Harry. I wonder what species they are?'

'Dunno. Those flashy coloured ones are parrots I think, but whatever, I'm sure they're all happy feeding on the flowers up there. I reckon it's the fantastic fragrances given off from those flowers that we smell occasionally that attract them.

'We've been lucky so far, Patrick; there's no shortage of water, or trackside feed for the horses. But mate, you should see the back of your shirt!'

'Why, pray tell?'

'Well, right now there's probably a few thousand of those bastard bush flies congregating on the back of your shirt. What do yah reckon; they're just along for a ride, or that they're after your manly sweat?'

'Very funny Harry, but your shirt's the same. I reckon they have it in for us and there's no point trying to whack them away, they just circle around before resettling. If you leave them alone though, far fewer seem intent upon getting into your eyes.

'Yeah, the little shits, they all seem determined to drive us and our horses to total distraction.'

At night, the bush flies were replaced by an even worse pest; swarms of bloodthirsty mosquitoes, resulting in little sleep, uncontrollable scratching from their bites and the loss of their normally even-temperament the following day.

But as good luck would have it, there were no sightings of bushrangers.

Viewed from afar while lounging in their saddles, Gloucester was obviously positioned to take advantage of a fertile valley at the foot of an impressive jump-up mountain range.

They were soon to realise Gloucester's rural businesses and township infrastructure were both well-developed, while retaining an easy informality... and word was out that the area was soon to be surveyed for a railway line, thus guaranteeing its ongoing prosperity.

* * *

IT WAS ONLY after Harry and Patrick had been in Gloucester for a month or so, while looking for replacement horses, that they discovered the whereabouts of their friend, Robert: not ten miles to the southwest of Gloucester where there was an expansive, undulating region of lightly timbered grassland.

Following the directions given to them by Gloucester's local butcher, they soon came to a well-fenced property carrying some sheep and several head of cattle. The cottage was built from a combination of local stone and machine-milled timber boards. The roof was corrugated iron. It also had a wrap-around verandah on three sides, glazed windows and a stone chimney with a wisp of smoke escaping from it. In fact, it was the complete antithesis of Robert's property at Frederickton.

As Harry and Patrick dismounted, the cottage door flew open and there stood Robert, unsmiling and with a shotgun loosely draped over his arm.

'I hope you closed the front fence gate before you... well, I'll be buggered,' Robert stammered in disbelief and excitement. 'I do believe it's young Harry and Lieutenant Patrick!'

'Yep, none other,' Harry and Patrick chimed in unison.

'And you won't need the shotgun Robert,' Harry quickly added as he returned Robert's handshake.

'I very seldom get any visitors, which generally suits me, but God Almighty, you two... I'd never have believed this,' Robert said ecstatically. 'Well, come on, let's get inside and have a cuppa; you both look like you need one and we've got loads to talk about, eh.'

Before stepping inside, Patrick warmly shook Robert's hand. 'So good to finally meet again. We damn nearly gave up; thought we'd lost yah.'

* * *

AFTER SEVERAL POTS of hot tea, a tin of sweet biscuits and much laughter, the men finally got round to talking about Robert's unexpected departure from Frederickton.

'It wasn't any one thing, but rather a succession of events,' Robert started to explain. 'At first, I was quite proud and excited that I had inherited what seemed to be an ideal sheep breeding property. But in fact, I've concluded that the inheritance was a rotten joke, or demented payback for something I was supposedly still responsible for back in England; but God only knows what.

'Regardless, the land transfer documents were official, but knowing what I do now I would have knocked back the property. My fault entirely, I should have asked more questions.

'Anyone for more tea before I press on? No-one? But be a good lad Harry and refill the kettle would you?'

When Harry put the kettle back on the wood stove, Robert resumed his story. 'After I said farewell to Alf and Jim, everything went downhill. First, as you've already seen, the cottage was on the verge of collapsing, most of the post and rail fencing had been nicked for firewood and the ground was saturated in many places, permanently I suspect.

'The following day, two drunken louts rode up yelling inane abuse... then started taking pot shots at my sheep! I was too far away to drop the bastards when I first challenged em, but I gave 'em something to think about when I fired just the one shot; it fortunately sent 'em off in a hurry. Bloody cowards! I'd really like to meet them without their guns. Sadly, the rotten bastards killed five of my best ewes and two of my rams.

'Incredibly, things got worse. That night, there was a huge thunderstorm and a massive downpour, which panicked the entire flock. They went in all directions looking for shelter, but in the morning I only managed to find twelve ewes and one of the rams. The poor buggers were saturated and really distressed.

'And to top everything off, about a week later, a pack of yellow dogs killed another two ewes. Native dogs: dingoes they're called. Beautiful animals, but not welcome. Mind you, they could have killed a lot more before leaving my sheep alone.

'Anyway, I found my way to Gloucester and with the last of my money I received for my Frederickton property and my sheep, I purchased this place. Well, technically, the bank owns it, but they've been most helpful, allowing me to buy the cattle and sheep you no doubt saw as you rode up to my cottage.'

'Well, good on you my friend, you seem to have landed on your feet,' said Patrick. 'But come on, how about you give us the grand tour?'

An hour later after returning to the cottage, Harry put his hand on Robert's shoulder and asked. 'Pray tell mate, do you recognise our horses?'

'Can't say that I do; should I?' Robert replied as he stared at his visitor's horses.

Ignoring Robert's question, Patrick asked quietly. 'And do you reckon you could describe those two idiots who shot your sheep?'

'Yes, I suppose I could,' Robert replied quizzically, 'but why the questions, that stuff's in the past and surely best forgotten?'

'Maybe,' replied Patrick, 'but first, let Harry and me describe them for you. Then I think we can tell you exactly where they are, and what's about to befall them.'

Five minutes later, Robert threw up his hands and said, 'Well I'll be buggered. That's a bloody amazing story and yes, that's them to a T... I'm certain.

'Serves the bastard's right and I hope they get at least ten years each.

'But boys please, don't tell me the Guvnor's horses that were stolen from him were then stolen by you two?'

'No way,' Patrick replied firmly, 'all three were gifted to us by the Guvnor for Harry's exemplary behaviour.'

17

Harry and Patrick stayed with Robert for nearly three months, repairing fencing, installing new gates, cutting and stacking firewood, assisting with crutching the sheep and collecting food and building materials from Gloucester. They even built a large, hawk-proof enclosure to house ten "at-the-point-of-laying" pullets.

However, the purchase of a Coolgardie safe was their priority; the second being to ensure a cool beer was always close to hand to farewell the passing of each day.

Robert's gratitude was genuine, but so was his frustration: regardless, his guests refused to accept any payment... for anything.

* * *

While stacking goods after a typical shopping trip, Patrick asked, 'I say, Robert, apart from those two clowns who shot your sheep, have you heard about any other bushrangers in this region; a bloke like Captain Thunderbolt, for example?'

'Oh, yes, indeed. I met him once at the pub in town, not long after I moved here. I only learned who he was later; he tried to sell me some horses and was just a bit pushy at first. Asked him if he had proof of ownership... which changed our conversation somewhat.'

'Yeah, I bet it did,' quipped Harry.

'Actually, he seemed quite relaxed and wasn't unpleasant at all. He chatted civilly with me while finishing his beer, before bidding me a cheerful farewell.

'Haven't seen him since. A couple of months before you two turned up, I heard from the local cop that the good captain had been shot dead and that his gang had since scattered. I guess that's what's called progress, eh?'

'You do realise, Robert, that if that had been me, I'd have been duty bound to either arrest him... or, to kill him?'

* * *

ON THE FIRST day it snowed—the first they had seen since leaving England— Patrick announced that he and Harry would soon be leaving for places unknown; again, probably south.

'You both must be mad,' replied Robert. 'Surely by now you should know it only gets colder the further south you travel. Besides, I've got some news that might interest you both.'

'Like what, pray tell?'

'I ran into my neighbour this morning: George, the Greek. Good bloke; honest and religious and all that but getting a bit long in the tooth. There's a small settlement not far from here, Copeland, it's called. Apparently, according to George, there's a gold mine there and it's being upgraded. Word's out that the mine owners are looking for strong young blokes, and that the money being offered is unbelievable.'

'What's that you're saying, Robert?' Harry asked with jovial inquisitiveness as he walked into the room where his friends had been chatting. 'You trying to get rid of us, or what?'

'No, not at all, you're both more than welcome to stay here for as long as you wish. I was just saying to Patrick you would both make perfect mine workers. You're both strong and not afraid of hard work and you both no doubt could do with a few more bob in your kitties... and I've been told all the jobs are extremely well-paid.

'Like I said, I just thought you might be interested.'

'Come on Harry it's probably exactly what we need. I'm not keen on freezing my nuts off while doing nothing,' Patrick added wisely.

'Ehhmm,' Harry responded. 'Sounds interesting. No harm done to check it out, I suppose.'

* * *

AN HOUR before daylight the next morning, Harry and Patrick had finished saddling their horses and loading their meagre belongings onto their packhorse.

Robert then called them in for a breakfast "fit for kings", as Harry later declared it: huge, perfectly grilled cuts of eye fillet, fried eggs and onion rings and slabs of buttered toast oozing local honey... and several mugs of hot, sweetened black tea.

'Well Robert, thanks for putting up with us but it's time we got a move on,' Patrick announced. 'Time has flown, eh, but it's been enjoyable beyond our best expectations. I just wish there was something we could leave you to remember us by.'

'I tell you what, Robert,' Harry quickly replied. 'If I ever pass this away again, I'll take you back to Trial Bay and get the Guvnor to give you ten minutes with each of those lousy bushrangers who attacked you and shot your sheep. Mind you, it's highly likely the Guvnor has already dished 'em both up with a wee bit of tap.'

'Thanks, but no need, Harry,' replied Robert. 'They've already lost the most important thing in their wretched lives, and that's their freedom.'

After parting handshakes and back patting, Patrick and Harry mounted their horses. 'We'll miss you, Robert,' said Patrick. 'Take care mate.'

'Likewise, lads. But hang on just a minute, I've forgotten something.'

When Robert returned from his cottage, he was carrying a single barrel shotgun and several boxes of ammunition. 'Here, Harry, you just might need this one day. I've no need for it; too bloody dangerous to have lying around. It's a beautiful old piece, an early Stevens, but there's a small problem with the cartridge ejection mechanism. Here, you'll need this too; just the right size to drop down the barrel to free up any offending cartridge that gets stuck.'

'Well thanks, Robert; a pocketknife, no less. Must be the smallest one I've ever seen. You sure you won't need it?'

'Nah, I think you'll need it more than me. Anyway, if you open the largest blade, you'll see my initials etched on it... RWE.'

With that, Harry and Patrick shook up their horses, waved in unison and without looking back headed for the front gate of Robert's property.

18

The track to Copeland was in reasonable repair, but it was evident something large, or of considerable weight, had recently passed in the direction Harry and Patrick were travelling; the giveaway being the fresh deep wheel ruts and the astonishing number of huge indentations of cloven hoof marks.

'This I've got to see,' said Patrick, 'there must be at least a dozen, or maybe even more bullocks pulling their guts out to move whatever the load is. Something connected with the mine upgrades would be my guess. C'mon, let's catch 'em up.'

At a gentle canter, half an hour later, they heard the bullock team before it came into sight. Most of their pursuit had been on a relatively gentle uphill gradient, but from Harry and Patrick's current vantage point above the bullock team, it was obvious what now confronted that team was very different; an abrupt, treacherous descent of about two hundred yards that eventually tapered off to level ground.

As Harry and Patrick rode up to the now stationary team, the load revealed itself—a huge metal drum of steel about three yards in diameter and six yards long. The load rested upon a sturdy, four-wheeled wooden wagon and was securely tied in place with several thick ropes.

Patrick's bullock estimate was way off. Not only were there sixteen in harness, connected to the wagon, but another sixteen were clearly enjoying a chance to forage nearby.

Out of curiosity, Harry and Patrick dismounted and introduced themselves to the driver and his offsider. It soon transpired that these men were a father and son team; Leo about sixty and Tom, perhaps in his mid-thirties. Both were tall, athletic and broad-shouldered and made no attempt to hide their masculine strength and baldness. And both were relaxed in the nonchalant manner of seasoned bushmen as they deftly attended to their roll-ups.

'Looks like you've got your hands full,' Patrick suggested amiably. 'What's your load and do you know its weight?'

'I'm told it's a boiler,' replied Leo as he lit his smoke and offered the flame to his son. 'For raisin' steam apparently, so that the boys at the gold mine can power their quartz crushin' machine what we bought up to Copeland about six weeks ago. Dunno its weight, but I'm told she's more than twelve ton. Just on our limit, like.'

'Wow. And you reckon you can get it down that slope without losing everything?' asked Harry.

'Yeah, we reckon so,' Tom replied in an undeterred, enthusiastic manner. We've done similar jobs up north, near Ellenborough. It'll be tricky, but I'll explain. Here, both of you, take a seat on this 'ere log and I'll explain.

'The reason we've pulled over is to give these boys a breather. They sure deserve it, that last few miles was all uphill; took the starch out of 'em a bit. Mind you, they're smart enough to let us know when they've had enough; they get grumpy like and start bellowin', or just stop pullin'.

'We'll give 'em another fifteen minutes then we'll start leadin' those other boys up and into line up front, two abreast of course. You'll soon catch on when yah see how it's done. You might even like to give us a hand with some of the other jobs.'

'What do you reckon Patrick?' Harry asked. 'We're in no hurry.'

'No problem,' Patrick answered. 'What can we do, Leo?'

'Well, the first thing we *must* do is extend that length of square section hardwood out from where it slides between runners under the wagon. It's called the drag-pole. It acts as a brake; uses friction and digs into the track if the slope starts gettin' too steep. I'll show you how to slip the lockin' pin into place to secure it, like.

'Then I'll get you both to run out that chain on the back of the wagon, but she's heavy. Don't be droppin' it on your foot.

'While you're doin' that, Tom and me'll start pushin' those other lazy buggers over there up to the front of the first team and start hookin' 'em into their traces.'

'Is that it?' Harry asked, somewhat confused and impatient. 'Surely that won't be enough to stop the wagon if she gets away a bit.'

'Hold your horses, young fella,' Leo replied. 'Come and have a look at this.' In unison the four men stood up from the log they had been sitting on and Leo walked over to the wagon's off-side rear wheel. Harry and Patrick quickly followed.

'See here? These are hardwood brake-blocks. Whoever's upfront can mechanically wind these down onto the wheel rim, as tight as needed, like. There's a handwheel up there. Got the same for the other back wheel. They're our main brakes.

'There's also another smaller set of block-brakes for the front wheels, but it's risky usin' 'em. If they get too tight, all the bloody wheels can lock-up and the wagon can start to skid, which ain't ideal. That's when you can lose good bullocks, broken legs and so on. It's never nice having to put 'em down, knowing how hard they've always worked for us.

'Anyway, that's not all. See that log we were just sittin' on? We need to tie it to the end of that chain you'll run out. Just hitch it somewhere around the middle of the log. We'll be dragging it behind us as we descend, and it'll play a big role in keeping our forward speed down to a minimum. There're enough branches coming from the log that'll stop the log from rollin' and the chain from rollin' up, like.'

'So, what about the bullocks; what are they doing?' Patrick asked. 'Don't they have to back-up somehow to do their bit? Like digging in their hooves to take the load? Is that why you're also hooking up all those other lads?'

'Well, yeah, that's sort of right,' said Leo patiently, 'but actually, there's only going to be four of 'em doin' the really hard stuff. They're the only ones that'll be connected direct via chains to the wagon. They're our strongest of course. When they're really working hard, you'll see their heads come up as if they're judging how far they have to go before getting their next breather.'

'But no whip, eh, not while all this is going on,' Harry said, part questioning, part demanding.

'No bloody way! Never on a downhill,' Leo and Tom chorused *very* firmly indeed.

* * *

THE DESCENT WAS BASICALLY UNEVENTFUL, other than for some outrageous profanities and colourful encouragement.

'Jesus H Christ, Bossman,' Tom yelled on top note, 'you're not here for your good looks. If yah don't start doin' your bit, I'll kick my right boot so far up your arse yah breath'll smell like boot polish!"

Not to be outdone, it seemed, Leo let fly with, 'By the Christ Almighty, Red, you really are a dopey bastard. Walk-up straight, or I'll strip every inch of hide off yah arse. By the geezes I hope yah mother loved yah, because I bloody well don't!'

By the time the wagon reached the bottom of the incline, it became obvious to Harry and Patrick why it was the second team of bullocks had been brought into play. Although the track levelled out, it wasn't long after that its gradient began to increase significantly again, just as the settlement of Copeland came into view.

As the wagon slowed, Tom and Harry quickly climbed aboard it and busily set about releasing the front and rear brakes. Leo and Patrick, walking behind, skilfully refitted the drag-pole beneath the wagon, then knocked the heavy metal pin free to release the log-towing chain from the wagon.

Though the wagon was moving, albeit quite slowly, Leo and Tom, now sporting long-handled whips, started rallying their entire team to take advantage of whatever forward momentum remained.

The air was suddenly ripped apart by the simultaneous *ker-rack, ker-rack* of well-placed whiplashes and a litany of equally well-practiced words of encouragement from Leo and Tom.

The bullock's response was immediate; almost in unison their heads went down and chains and traces were snapped tight as most of the team stepped forward, throwing all their remaining strength into their hauling harnesses.

The wagon continued forward, still slow at first, but then gradually faster until finally settling on a steady, manageable pace. A few bellows of protest continued from those beasts who had been caught napping at the initial weight take up.

As the wagon trundled on, Harry and Patrick pulled the drag-log from the track. They then bundled up the drag chain and as requested by Leo and Tom, left it track-side for them to collect on their homeward journey.

Arriving at the settlement, Harry and Patrick were pleased to see that a small crowd had gathered to greet the waggoneers and their huge bullocks. 'Thanks for your help, lads,' Leo called to them, 'much appreciated. We'll catch up later for a beer or two, eh?'

<h1 style="text-align:center">19</h1>

Surprisingly, accommodation was simple for Harry and Patrick to locate. It was just a case of riding around the settlement until they agreed upon the house that appealed to them most. Typically, signs on display read:-

Mine workers welcome

Cash only

Free clothes washing

Horse yard with stables extra

Enquire within

The house they chose was old but comfortable, with a lounge and fireplace and a well-appointed kitchen with a wood-burning oven. There were also separate bedrooms, both with curtained windows overlooking most of the settlement and importantly, provided a commanding view of both tracks leading into it. A covered verandah surrounded the cottage on three sides and a table and two old wicker chairs were strategically placed adjacent to the front door.

The owners were old folk who had a second property nearby, to where they would retreat after Harry and Patrick paid their bond and moved in. But not before the old man asked, 'You boys stayin' long, or just movin' through, like? If you're lookin' for work, the word is that there's any amount available at the mine. She's called the Mountain Maid Gold Mine by the way. And if you're any good, the wages are ridiculous, I'm told.'

'Thank you, sir,' replied Patrick, 'we'll probably stay on for some time if we can get jobs. If not, we'll probably be gone in a week or so.'

'You'll be alright, boys, just ask to see the mine supervisor, 'is name's Clive, Clive Lord. Not a bad bloke I can tell yah, provided yah don't upset 'im. He's about fifty and carryin' a bit of weight, always smok'n a pipe, goin' bald and lives 'ere with his wife and two kids. Ah well, gotta go. Be sure to look after our home or me missus will gut both of yah.

'By the way, weather's been closin' in lately, so you'll soon need to cut heaps more firewood; you're sure going to need it.

'And you'll need to be thinkin' about organisin' some hay for your horses. There might be a pick for 'em nearby for a while, but that'll die back to nothin' pretty soon, I'd say.'

* * *

'WELL THAT WAS BLOODY EASY,' said Harry as he and Patrick walked side by side from the mine site, delighted at their successful quest for work. 'Don't like the idea of workin' underground, but for those sorts of wages I reckon I could get to like it. I'll tell you what though, I won't be doin' that for the rest of my life; that'd be even worse than being inside.'

'That's definitely not for me either, me being a man raised on the oceans and having excelled at ship provisioning,' Patrick replied with a smirk. 'Mind you, my British Navy ranking and service papers must have impressed Clive, apart from my enthusiasm and good demeanour, of course.

'Regardless, Clive's not a bad sort, but how about him giving *me* the Supply Manager's job, when he really doesn't know me from a bull's foot? That, therefore, makes *me* second in charge, so you'd better not start giving me any grief Harry, my good man.

'He even suggested I order anything we might need through the company... including hay and so forth for our horses. We should be well placed soon enough to buy our own cart, so in the meantime if anyone asks who's paying the haulage, we tell them nothing. For us, it's just one of those things called a silent bonus, or a perk.

'Anyway, were you listening when Clive told us about that Saxby chap? I take it from your apparent lack of eagerness that you weren't. Anyway, that fellow was the first to discover gold in this district, not that long ago actually, in '76 I think Clive said.

'Apparently, he was a timber cutter looking for highly prized red cedar trees, but instead fell upon nuggets of gold in the Copeland Creek, which runs close to this township. After his discovery, the dopey twit started crowing about his good fortune, so word soon got out and miners from everywhere have been converging on this place in ever increasing numbers ever since.

'In fact, Clive reckons that building over there next to that giant gum is about to become the first pub. And directly across the road where those chaps are working now, putting in stumps, I think they'll become the first of eight different stores planned to create self-reliance for that anticipated huge influx of gold-hungry folk.

'Clive was also very excited the plans to build a post office and a school have been approved; and heaven forbid, those for a six-cell jail.

'Regardless, Harry, we'll know soon enough when it's time to move on, eh?'

20

Both men threw themselves into the challenge of learning their respective jobs.

Harry first had to overcome the claustrophobia and appalling low light level that almost sent him screaming from the mine on more than one occasion.

Second, being over six feet tall, his head often unexpectedly found the tunnel's roof support beams, which either left him dazed and down on his knees, or in a colourful rant, trumped only by the repertoire used by the bullock teamsters he'd met the week before.

Third, being "bent over like a half open pocket-knife all day", as he often complained, wasn't doing Harry's lower back any favours.

Fourth, though he hated it, he soon found it necessary to always wear a large neckerchief to avoid swallowing and inhaling the ever-present rock dust.

And fifth, he never did find a way of avoiding the built-up stale air which often left him dizzy from his exertions and which demanded a hasty retreat to the outdoors. This was to become an escalating, real and life-threatening hazard, which only got worse as the tunnel network penetrated deeper into the mountain.

But Harry had never been a quitter. Yes, it was hard work being underground winning the precious gold-bearing quartz, shoring up the tunnels and extending the wooden tracks for the ore trucks.

Nevertheless, he was also a fast learner. Within a month Harry had unintentionally glorified himself in a form of adulation. He was not only leading all other miners in the number of filled ore carts per day but had all but taken over the task of selecting, cutting and hauling timber back to the mine. Of course, most off-cuts found their way to the woodshed where he lived.

During this time, Harry also helped to install and commission the new steam raising boiler for the ore crushing plant. Its instant success was broadly heralded as the heart of the entire gold mining venture... as it was intended to be for the next decade.

As for Patrick, his commercial acumen was put to the test. A budget did not exist and astonishingly, Clive had not yet employed an accountant. After a quick inspection of receipts, it was soon obvious to Patrick that costs to date far exceeded income, any income! However, Patrick soon had both sides of a ledger under a semblance of being quantified and understood, which pleased Clive no end and put him at ease.

Pragmatic plans were immediately necessary to safeguard the fortune that was now being won, because without realising that wealth, the company would soon be broke and the mine would be forced to close.

During that time, Patrick accompanied Clive into Gloucester to meet with a large group of creditors to reassure them their patience regarding overdue payment was greatly appreciated and that those outstanding payments would soon be honoured... immediately after the Mountain Maid Gold Mine received payment for the imminent first gold consignment to the State Government coffers.

When Patrick was given the floor, he added with good humour, aplomb and sincerity that each creditor would receive a substantial *ex-gratia* payment as appreciation for their patience.

Applause followed; but had those folk been looking at Clive, rather than at Patrick, they would have seen Clive's face transform from calm to total perplexity as the shock of Patrick's unexpected announcement sank in. The poor man's eyes and mouth were now wide open and his lips quivered as he tried to form the words of protest he so wanted to scream.

* * *

ABOUT HALF A MILE out of Gloucester, their horses at an easy canter, an exasperated Clive suddenly broke the silence and hissed. 'Geezus, Patrick! What the hell have you done? I didn't authorise that! Are you mad, or what?'

'Not mad, Clive; you saw their faces when I started my little speech,' Patrick replied calmly. 'They were about ready to lynch you. And you also saw their faces when we left: all in a good frame of mind, feeling secure... and every one of them happy to provide an ongoing line of credit.'

Silence followed. After a few minutes Clive turned in his saddle to look at Patrick. Sensing this, Patrick returned his gaze. A smile creased Clive's face. Harry returned his smile, then broke into a chuckle.

Clive suddenly threw back his head and roared with laughter, startling his horse, which began pig-rooting; back arched, ears back and all four hooves off the ground. Clive was promptly unseated and airborne, but luckily, though he landed on his backside, was unhurt.

Though slightly winded, Clive could not stop laughing, so hard in fact, that he had to look away from Patrick who was now mimicking a hangman placing a noose around someone's neck. Finally, Clive composed himself enough to say, 'by Christ, Patrick, you're a clever bloody rogue... but thanks, anyway.'

'I'll go and get your horse, Clive, then let's get serious for a moment, eh? We must discuss security at the mine, it's practically nonexistent and at the same time it's essential we make plans to get a meaningful shipment of gold to the authorities, and soon, or our good creditors will be after us to do more than just shake our hands.

'Look, Clive, I've got a few ideas that might help,' said Patrick with implied authority as he passed the reins of Clive's horse back to him. 'But regardless, I want Harry in on this. You'll need to include a few of your most important men in whatever we discuss, but only those you can trust. And Clive, you'll have to sign off on everything that's agreed. Alright?'

21

Over the following few weeks, Harry and Patrick made it a pleasant habit at the end of each working day to sit on the old wicker chairs on the front verandah of their cottage and imbibe in either a hot cup of tea, or if the mood grabbed them, a cool beer. Occasionally, neighbours would call in for a chat. Most others who walked by would raise a hand to acknowledge them, whereupon Harry and Patrick would call out their names and typically either enquire after their health, or how their kids were getting on at school.

One evening, out of the blue, Patrick said to Harry, 'has anyone told you that those magnificent mountains to our west are called the Barrington Tops?'

'Yeah, apparently the locals call 'em "tops" because once you get to the top, you can only go down; a bit corny, I know. On the other hand, most reckon there's good summer grazing to be had up there for their cattle.

'Also, according to other locals in the know, the Barrington Tops were named after Lord Barrington, but no one knows which Lord Barrington because apparently the family has no connection with Australia. Strange, eh?

'It's also said by some that the wilderness surrounding us here hides pristine rivers and some massive gorges with amazing waterfalls. Dunno why, but they nevertheless call this area a *dry* rainforest. That's a bit strange too, I reckon.' Regardless, we've gotta see it, eh?'

'Agreed. Sounds like we must go and have a good look around. But before we do, do you think your local friends might know if another track leads on to Gloucester without going over the tops, or through the settlement of Barrington? In fact Harry, that's your job for tomorrow.'

'Can do, but why is it that I'm suddenly feeling uneasy? You're up to something, I just know it!'

'All in good time, Harry. C'mon, our stew smells like it's about ready; you're starving again I suppose?'

* * *

LATER THAT NIGHT, well after the mine's battery stamper and air compressor had been shut down and no more raised voices or the sound of children playing could be heard, Patrick ushered Harry into the lounge room and adjusted their fuel lamp to radiate a full but relaxing light.

'Get comfortable Harry, I've got some news that could well change our lives forever. It could mean that we'll both become very rich and never again have to raise a sweat, so to speak.

'Mind you, my loyal and adventurous friend, there are considerable risks involved, which, if things go wrong, might see us both inside for the term of our natural lives. But you're under no obligation to join me in what I've got planned, but I sure could use your help. If you choose not to get involved, I need your word that you'll say nothing about this conversation... ever!'

'Shit! I knew it. This really *is* serious stuff I take it?'

'Yes. Opportunity always is.'

'Well, I can't give you my answer until I bloody well know what the hell you've got in mind, can I? So come on Patrick... spit it out!'

'Before I get started, do you recall the conversation we had with

Clive regarding security at the mine and our preparations for shipment of the first gold consignment?'

'Yes of course. Why?'

'What do you make of those two men handpicked by Clive as his most honest and trustworthy employees; apart from us of course?'

'You mean Ron Viner and Teddy Green? They didn't have much to say, but they seemed straight enough and genuinely interested in our plans. Though, thinking about it, that Teddy Green can be an irritable bastard; always seems to have a chip on his shoulder. God only knows why. And... you've probably noticed he's totally devoid of any sense of humour.

'Viner seems more normal, like. And he loves talking about how good he is with horses.

'Apart from that I've got no idea where they come from.'

'Ehhm, but would you trust them? What do you know of their former lives? And *I know for a fact* that Clive has no paperwork to justify the faith he's placed in their selection as trustees: he's been conned, Harry!

'And yes, of course they paid close attention to what we've planned... because, Harry, my friend, *they intend to steal that first shipment!*'

'Ah come on, that's utter bullshit!' Harry replied incredulously as he jumped up from his chair.

'Easy now Harry. Please, sit down. That's not only the truth, but it's also only half of what I need to tell you.'

Obviously intrigued, Harry reluctantly sat, while asking, 'How on earth could you possibly know they intend to knock off that consignment? It'll be guarded by troopers.'

'Yes it will, but how would you like to turn your hand to a bit of unorthodox bush rangerin'... just for a few days? You see Harry, no one will ever suspect us of stealing back that gold from Ron and Teddy, would they? I'm convinced that Clive and all the locals we know here trust us unquestioningly, just by us being our good selves. No one will have any idea where the gold has gone once it's in our possession, except us and we might even get the credit for

Ron and Teddy's arrest... for the initial theft that *they* intend to execute.'

Totally bewildered, Harry slumped back into his seat. 'I think you've gone nuts, but you'll have to give me a lot more detail before I make up my mind. For one, no matter what transpires, I'm not going back inside. And won't we be betraying Clive and our friends here?'

'Understood. And yes, we will. But on balance you may later see things differently. All will now be revealed, then tell me if I've gone nuts. But first, I'll put the kettle on for a cuppa; you want one?'

* * *

THE CONVERSATION THAT NIGH DID, in fact, set the course of their lives forever.

For example, neither Harry nor Patrick ever learned why Teddy Green had such an unpleasant disposition. Of course, they knew nothing of his upbringing, the youngest child in a seriously poor and dysfunctional family of five... and forever it seemed to him, never loved and that he would never own anything of value.

Saddened and depressed, his only view on life was to survive by simply grabbing whatever he could and care not a tinkers toss if his actions disappointed anyone, or everyone.

Nor could they have ever foreseen Teddy's ruthless determination to get what he believed was rightfully his.

* * *

FOR THE NEXT hour or so, Patrick detailed his plan, and though Harry interjected on a few matters of detail, he eventually said. 'Alright Patrick, I'm in, but only if Robert agrees to come on board.'

'It's our day off tomorrow, so I think we should be paying him a visit. If he wants in, then he gets a third of the gold. If he refuses to join us, all bets are off and we abandon our plan. Fair enough?'

'Just one more question Patrick. How *did* you learn that Ron and Teddy were up to no good?'

'Fate, Harry! Simply fate.

'As you know, both occasionally work in the same administration building as me. About ten days ago after I had returned from the long drop, I could hear some chaps talking. The walls of that admin building are as thin as a cigarette paper; that's why it's always so damn cold inside.

'Anyway, I placed my ear against the wall on the inside of the building as if I was catching some warmth that had penetrated it... and heard everything that's worth knowing about *their* plans. Listening carefully, I easily recognised those two. Stupid twats: all they needed to do was walk about twenty yards into the scrub and I would never have known anything of their evil intentions... and we'd not be having this conversation.

'It's paramount from now on Harry, that we say *absolutely nothing* to anyone about what we know, except Robert of course. And we can't act as if we might know something's up. Be yourself but keep any explanations or questions to a minimum.

'Just keep in mind Harry, my good man, the three of us can't be hung for relieving stolen goods that were previously nicked by thieving bushrangers! Particularly if those goods never surface to become evidence.'

Shaking his head in disbelief Harry walked into his bedroom and closed the door.

Smiling to himself, Patrick snuffed out the lounge room lamp, then said quietly, 'Ehhmm, that went well.'

22

———————

Over the following few days, final preparations for the first gold shipment from the Mountain Maid Gold Mine were discussed and agreed by the management team. Ron and Teddy were always in attendance and not backwards in seeking clarifications. Only Patrick and Harry noticed the occasional meaningful glance between them.

Outwardly, Ron was an affable type: tall, thin and slightly stooped. He was generally well groomed and sported a full, bushy, red beard. And he was always on for a chat, so long as *he* was talking most of the time.

Teddy too was as thin as a whippet, never well-groomed and his jet-black beard, greying in places, was bordering on unsightly. The most common response from Teddy was a dismissive grunt... if you were lucky.

* * *

At week's end as previously notified, two government troopers, Jonathon Boyd and Matthew Rogers, arrived at the mine site whereupon Jonathon immediately presented their identification and authorisations papers to Clive. Both visitors were dressed in the fashion of farmers, 'to minimise attracting unwanted attention,' Jonathon confided.

After introductions all round, the five men then toured the mine site, even though Jonathon expressed his main interest lay in ensuring all was in readiness for transferring the gold to Newcastle.

He was not fazed that this consignment would be in raw nugget and spec form, rather than in ingots, which explained why both men carried well-used, unremarkable looking saddle bags.

By the time Jonathon and Matthew were shown to their overnight accommodation, Patrick and Harry were finally privy to which return route the government men would take, and when... but so too were Ron and Teddy!

* * *

AN HOUR AFTER NIGHTFALL, Patrick and Harry saddled up and took the minor road that led away from Copeland, the one which Harry had earlier learnt bypassed most of the main road back to Gloucester. Just as Harry had reported back to Patrick, this road needed repair in places, but was otherwise wide enough for two riders side by side, or for a medium-sized wagon to pass without too much fear or inconvenience.

After passing through Gloucester at a sedate pace, they then rode hard to Robert's farm, where they spent an hour or so updating him of their final plans, before retiring.

All three men were wide awake, dressed in typical farmer's working garb and had finished the breakfast which Robert had prepared for them just as the false dawn flooded over the farmhouse and surrounding countryside. Not much was spoken: the mood was subdued but tinged with excitement. Having rechecked their firearms and ammunition belts, Harry and Patrick were soon back in their saddles and pushing their steeds towards the front gate of Robert's property.

Robert, in Patrick and Harry's recently acquired wagon would follow, albeit giving them a thirty-minute head start. His job was to arrive at an agreed position and stay there, out of sight, until he heard gun shots; the strategy being that he would immediately advance over the crest in the road to become *an independent witness* to the anticipated holdup activities. However, his additional intervention would only be necessary if his friends appeared to be in peril of being overpowered.

Knowing that the government troopers would also be leaving Copeland with their precious cargo at dawn, Patrick had calculated the night before—with some degree of precision, he assured himself —exactly where and when they would arrive at the most likely holdup location.

Patrick also had no doubt that Ron and Teddy were reasonably smart and likely to come to the same conclusion as himself, for the location recalled by Patrick was perfect: uphill for any approaching riders, sun in their eyes and the road bordered on both sides by huge gum trees and dense undergrowth.

Unwittingly and naively, Teddy had let it slip at one of the mine management meetings that he preferred "the backroad because it was a short cut to Gloucester and far more scenic".

This strongly implied to Patrick that the would-be robbers needed to be in position themselves, out of sight and well before the arrival of the troopers. This meant that he and Harry had to be in an equally favourable location *before* Ron and Teddy turned up, which, in turn meant that he and Harry were now obliged to push their ageing horses extremely hard to fulfil their initial role as "observers", albeit only until both robbers had fled with the gold.

* * *

PATRICK AND HARRY dismounted and each then led their horse about one hundred yards up the hill on one side of the road, then tethered them. Armed, they then scrambled down the hill and found positions close to the roadside, which enabled them to see each other, but where they could not be seen from the road.

They had barely settled when Harry signalled to Patrick that two riders were approaching: clearly it was Ron and Teddy for few men had such unforgettable red hair and matching beard as did Ron.

The would-be robbers dismounted about twenty yards past where Patrick and Harry were concealed, then quickly led their horses into the bush, taking up positions on either side of the road, though they both kept their horses close to hand.

Patrick immediately flashed his hand in the agreed fashion, reminding Harry to stay put until the robbery was executed and the robbers had fled... and that only then would he and Harry break cover to hunt down Ron and Teddy and relieve them of the gold.

The four men had to wait another twenty minutes before the troopers finally came into sight, at which time, no doubt in excitement, one of the robbers farted so loudly that their ensuing chuckles almost jeopardised their well-planned element of surprise.

Jonathon and Matthew rode calmly by the would-be robbers' position, but suddenly, urgently reined in their horses: both had just seen fresh hoofprints leading from the road.

What followed blew the best laid plans of all three parties into complete and utter chaos.

Jonathon quickly reached for his gun as he glimpsed Ron, not five yards behind, crashing his way through the undergrowth and onto the road. Both men fired simultaneously. Jonathon attempted another shot but instead, slid from his saddle and landed with a thump on the road, his face horribly disfigured, and the front of his vest already soaked in blood.

Ron's shot missed Jonathon, but purely by chance, hit Matthew. His plight too, was obviously dire for he also lay on his back on the road, blood oozing from the side of his mouth, legs occasionally twitching and both hands also clutching the front of his blood-soaked jacket.

Not only did all the birds in the vicinity leave their perches in raucous disapproval of the harsh noise, but so too did Teddy's horse react to the unexpected gunshots. In fright, it bucked savagely, sending Teddy sprawling onto his hands and knees beside the road.

Winded, Teddy gamely attempted to stand, but in another flurry of ill temper his horse again lashed out, its hooves this time collecting him flush on the side of his head.

In this state of confusion and disbelief, the ever-quick-thinking Ron, grabbed the saddle-bags from Jonathon's and Matthew's horses, raced back into the bush, threw the saddle bags over his horse's rump, swung into his saddle and not so expertly, furiously urged his horse up the hill to make good his escape.

Having heard the gunfire, Robert drove the wagon as fast as he could down the road. What confronted him was a scene of devastation, nothing like what he'd expected. Patrick and Harry were standing in the middle of the road holding the reins of their horses, heads down, peering at three lifeless, bloodied bodies.

'*Good God Almighty, what have you two done!*' Robert yelled at his shocked and disbelieving friends when the wagon came to an abrupt stop.

Patrick was the first to recover. 'Not us Robert; it's not what you might think mate. I'll try and explain, but it won't be easy: it just happened so unpredictably, and so bloody quick, like. There's nothing we can do for the poor buggers; they're all dead.'

'Here, you two better drink some of this,' said Robert, 'local brandy, should pick you up a bit. Hang on, where's Harry?'

<h1 style="text-align:center">23</h1>

Incensed by the carnage he'd witnessed, Harry angrily mounted his horse and slipped away into the scrub, leaving Robert and Patrick to seriously mull over the disaster.

Driven by an intense, almost maniacal desire to capture and punish Ron, Harry followed in the general direction he thought his foe had taken and soon, albeit luckily given the thick undergrowth, crossed a path of recently broken saplings and tree branches. Unexpectedly, Harry noticed something snagged on one of those branches: standing out like a beacon, was a small piece Ron's familiar black shirt for sure.

After another twenty minutes or so, this time movement through the undergrowth ahead caught Harry's eye. He dismounted, grabbed his shotgun and approached cautiously.

No sign of Ron. But his horse was on the ground, thrashing around in pain and clearly distressed at not being able to stand. Both saddle bags lay beside the horse, one of which partially concealed the extent of its hideously fractured lower front leg and a severe laceration from which huge volumes of the horse's blood spurted rhythmically.

Although Harry knew euthanasia was the moral thing to do, that notion was overridden by the fact that Ron was still missing, armed and potentially still very dangerous.

Harry sat with the dying horse for a while, cradling its head and stroking its face, but then inexplicably felt the need relieve himself. He stood and walked to the side of a steep drop off, not far in front of where Ron's horse had come to grief.

He stood admiring the majestic view of distant mountain tops, enjoying the relief to his bladder. Mid-stream, he lowered his eyes to gaze upon the canopies of the gum trees below, enjoying the sound and sight of their rustling leaves.

For no particular reason Harry lowered his eyes even further. Aghast, he suddenly knew what had happened to Ron, for there he was, about four or five yards below... wedged almost theatrically in the fork of a tree.

The unlucky robber had obviously been catapulted from his saddle and sent flying over the embankment; his back obviously breaking on impact and blood still oozing from his mouth and nose.

Consumed by this horrific sight Harry jumped in fright as one of Ronnie's legs involuntarily twitched in a death spasm, thus upsetting Harry's balance and still urgent flow so that urine splashed all over his fumbling hands and the front of his trousers.

'Ahhrr, shit and buggery!' Harry swore on top note.

Looking back at Ron's now deceased horse, it became clear to Harry what had happened here. He could envisage Ron mercilessly flogging his horse and his horse then unexpectedly baulking upon seeing the approaching drop off. The skid marks ploughed by Ron's horse while desperately trying to avoid injury were now obvious, as was the previously part-buried branch that had caused the hapless horse to trip and break its foreleg.

Now composed, with most of his anger under control, Harry picked up both saddlebags and checked their contents. All four leather bags of stolen gold were intact. 'Ehm, I can't risk being seen with this lot,' Harry muttered, 'and I can't bloody-well take it back with me.'

Scratching his head, he then hastily looked around and asked himself, 'Right, so where the hell *am* I supposed to hide this bloody stuff?'

* * *

BY THE TIME Harry caught up with his friends, they were within just a few miles of Copeland. Patrick was leading three horses, those previously owned by troopers Boyd and Rogers and bushranger Teddy Green.

Robert and Patrick stopped, grateful that Harry was unharmed and listened somewhat in awe as Harry laid bare his pursuit and recovery of the gold.

All three bodies had been moved to the side of the road and left there, discreetly covered with a tarpaulin; Patrick's rationale being that the police would insist upon investigating the scene, formally identifying the victims and confirming the cause of their deaths.

'I don't have to tell you both that all this changes our initial plans somewhat,' Patrick announced, 'but not that much if you think about it rationally.

'As Lady Luck would have it, we three are the only witnesses to what happened back there. Our story, I believe, should be exactly like this; it's simple and credible. We just all need to be singing the same song... and stick to it, no matter what. Besides, we surely can't be arrested, jailed or hung for *not* killing those men!

'Alright Harry, you must insist you have no idea where the saddle-bags went. After all, you spent considerable time looking for them and found nothing! Right?

'And Robert, the reason you were with us today was that Harry and I were simply accompanying you back to Copeland after you had finished repairs to our wagon at your farm; *and* so that we could introduce you to Clive in the hope that we could get you a job supplying meat to the townsfolk. You both happy to stick with that?

'There's bound to be a further search by the Gloucester copper and by the locals for the missing saddle-bags and for Ron's body. Government officials will no doubt also want to get involved.

'Harry, I'll tag along with you as a witness when those officials accompany you to locate Ron's body, and that of his horse: that discovery will be compelling evidence supporting our story.'

'Understood and agreed. But don't concern yourselves you two, nobody will ever find those saddle-bags without me,' Harry added quickly.

* * *

STATEMENTS WERE TAKEN. Ron's body was recovered, not without considerable difficulties given its state of decomposition. The horse remained where it had died.

However, when the Gloucester police first arrived at the scene, there were only two bodies beneath the tarpaulin: Teddy Green's body was missing!

'How the hell can that be?' Harry fumed, 'Teddy was stony dead when we left him. He couldn't have *just up and walked away!*'

'Officer, we *all* saw Teddy get kicked square in the head by his horse. Not a pretty sight, I can tell you.'

'Well, Harry, he aint here now,' the police officer replied dispassionately. 'I suggest that you boys might like to revise your statements.'

Patrick and Robert were equally astonished and bereft of any logical explanation for this mystery, but all three steadfastly stuck to their prearranged account of events.

24

But there *was* an explanation, albeit one Harry and Patrick would never have considered possible.

Whilst on a prolonged annual walkabout to resume contact with her mother's birthland and other members of her extended family, Yarran and her husband were by an amazing coincidence trekking nearby. Both had clearly heard gunshots and to satisfy their curiosity set off to investigate.

When they exited the scrub and stumbled upon the Gloucester back-road, they saw several drying pools of blood and in the mid-distance, three white men sitting shoulder to shoulder on a small wagon, leading five horses and heading away, north toward Copeland.

At the roadside, they also found three bodies beneath a green tarpaulin: two were dead and in the early stages of rigor mortis. The third person, though badly wounded and saturated in blood, was still alive... just!

Though not twenty years old, Yarran had witnessed many atrocities inflicted upon her people. She also wore multiple welts from being mercilessly whipped by a white man, for no other reason than she was begging for food for her ageing relatives.

However, she had also experienced inclusiveness and caring treatment from the Trial Bay community Governor and recalled with affection her time spent in the company of Harry and Patrick, both at sea and later, on land.

But right then, Yarran was overcome by an innate need to save the injured man's life, for he had done no wrong in her eyes and therefore his life was as important as her own.

With dedicated help from her husband, they found shelter for Teddy, fed him and nursed him to good health, at least to a stage where he could stand and attend to his toileting unaided. His injury, just below his left ear, had been significant. Though the bruising surrounding the wound site was healing quickly, the injury was no longer life threatening.

Three weeks later, Yarran and her husband successfully hailed a white family passing by in their ox-drawn cart. They were sympathetic toward Teddy's plight and whisked him away to the Gloucester hospital. True to form, Teddy expressed no appreciation whatsoever to Yarran and her husband for saving his life.

Soon after his arrival at the hospital, he was arrested for his role in the Copeland Mine gold heist. After two weeks of hospital attention, he was unceremoniously relocated to the Gloucester lockup and then extensively interrogated.

Teddy admitted to his involvement, but not to killing anyone. However, he refused to acknowledge knowing the other parties involved, nor could he be coerced into describing them, or their horses... or what became of the gold.

Teddy, it seemed to most, had become seriously demented: shuffling about, mumbling to himself and frequently spitting at his jail hosts. However, known only to Teddy, that apparent incurable mental condition was a successful charade designed to keep him away from the gallows. Fundamentally though, he just needed to stay alive for when, eventually, he was released... to then execute the long-term plan he fantasized.

It was initially decided by the travelling magistrates that Teddy's punishment would be ten years imprisonment. Regardless, he was determined to stay motivated to deliver on his main plan: to seek lethal revenge upon Harry and Patrick and to regain the stolen gold, all of it... and be rich! After all, he had by now convinced himself that that gold had been fated to be his, and only his!

Two years into his incarceration, a new member of the New South Wales Criminal Investigation Squad paid Teddy a most unexpected visit. The investigator's name was Mike Dudley, a polite, intelligent, enthusiastic and fit-looking young man in his mid-twenties.

Inspector Dudley quickly explained he was empowered to offer Teddy an early release in exchange for meaningful information about *"two other characters of interest who were probably involved in the Copeland gold theft"*.

'Unless you release me immediately,' Teddy insisted, 'you'll never find them.'

Two months later, Teddy Green was released and deemed a free man, albeit he became the total responsibility of Inspector Dudley.

25

———————

The saddle-bags of stolen gold were never found despite four extensive searches, and all three incredibly unlucky men were respectfully buried in the burgeoning Copeland graveyard.

No charges were laid. No subsequent accusations surfaced. Unanswered questions melted away... and Robert was given a highly valued meat supply contract serving Copeland's voracious populace.

Ever stoic, Clive addressed the Copeland community, reminding them that although the gold was not a king's fortune and probably an amount that would not pacify all creditors he still, however, felt that although the balance of creditors would be accepting of the loss, their patience and benevolence would nevertheless be well tested.

Regardless, life returned to something like normal at the Mountain Maid Gold Mine. Harry and Patrick again threw themselves into their work; respect for their "discovery" of the dead men further enhancing their reputations. And incredibly, their wages increased in lock-step with an increase in gold production.

Half a year flew by, then out of the blue, Patrick casually asked Harry, 'where too now, my friend? I've had enough of this existence.'

'I know I've said this before, but mate, you're a bloody mind reader. My back's giving me hell and I've had a gutful of meeting ever increasing payload outputs. So yeah, how about we continue south? Which means we won't have to endure another winter.'

'So, who's the mind reader now,' eh?'

* * *

CLIVE RECEIVED Patrick's announcement with his customary aplomb and sadness, regretting their decision to move on but wishing them both well, no matter where they might venture. The townsfolk, who knew them as good friends, chipped in and purchased for each of them a magnificent swag complete with overhead, protective mosquito mesh.

* * *

WITH PACKHORSE IN TOW, they soon arrived at the site of the "Copeland back road." Patrick asked quietly. 'So Harry, we now collect the gold... yes?'

'No, not here, at Robert's farm. I recovered the saddle bags a few weeks after the fourth community search, then hid 'em in his feed shed. He knows they're there. I just wanted to give you a surprise.'

'Well, I'll be buggered, on both counts. But pray tell, where the hell *did* you originally hide the saddle bags?'

'It occurred to me that if I hid 'em at ground level anywhere near by, in a cave or in a hollow log for example, that the cops or the locals would soon find 'em, regardless of how well I might *actually* hide 'em.

'So I asked myself, where *wouldn't* they look? At that time, I was gazing over a gully where there was a thick stand of gum trees with huge canopies.

'*Up!*' Harry pointed with a comical flourish. 'No one ever looks *up* when they're looking for treasure. So I climbed one of those trees as high as I dared and tied both saddle bags as tight as I could around its trunk.

'It worked, eh? No one found 'em' before I so athletically and daringly reclaimed 'em.'

'It worked, eh? No one found 'em' before I so athletically and daringly reclaimed 'em.'

26

When Patrick and Harry arrived at Robert's farm there was no shortage of smiles, handshakes, laughing, back patting and "liquid" celebration.

But no matter how persuasively Patrick and Harry tried, Robert refused to accept his share of the gold. 'Besides, you can't divide three into four and get an even amount,' replied Robert, trying to make light of his refusal. 'But I'll tell you what. If I ever fall into shitter's ditch, I'll let you know and you can send me a few quid.'

This seemed to placate Harry, but not so, Patrick, who replied, 'And just how, my friend, will you do that?'

'Good God, man,' Robert said with earnest intent, albeit while trying not to laugh. 'I'll just keep reading the newspaper headlines or check on the inmate's roll at the Trial Bay Jail from time to time.' That did it, for the onus was now clearly on Patrick and Harry to stay in touch with their faithful friend.

The following week, rested and reprovisioned, Harry and Patrick bade farewell.

* * *

RATHER THAN HEADING SOUTH, they chose to travel west across The Great Dividing Ranges to not only witness the high-country grazing plains of the Barrington Tops, but to visit some of its remotest surrounding natural wonders.

They gazed in awe at the steepness of huge valleys and at the waterfalls which cascaded in sheets into those valleys leaving thick shrouds of mist for miles downstream.

By consensus, they chose to camp on high ground with great views of the valleys, but where rocky outcrops provided protection from the wind. They both loved the magic of the early morning panoramas; when low clouds poured over the distant mountain ridges, when the kookaburras launched into their strange rounds of laughter and when the first updrafts of the day gently rustled the canopies of the trees in the valleys below.

THREE WEEKS later they arrived in Scone, predominantly a sheep grazing region, but with many fine-looking horses and a scattering of beef cattle.

Accommodation was easy to obtain, albeit about two miles west of the town centre, where they took over a small farm recently vacated by an ageing "squatter" couple.

THROUGH BOREDOM, not the need for cash, both men soon found employment repairing and extending dingo fences in the area to protect burgeoning flocks of sheep. 'You know what, Harry?' said Patrick as they sat eating their lunch during a noontime break. 'All the dingoes we've seen to date are magnificent creatures you'll have to agree. Most are that unusual sandy colour, but the odd one here and there are all black. How about the fearless way they strut about; proud heads held high, ears pricked and their feathery-like tails held up high, all belligerent like. And always alert.

'What I don't get is why all the sheep owners want to shoot, trap or poison the poor buggers. They were here first and I reckon a lot of farmers are making too much of them *supposedly* slaughtering their sheep. And the fool farmers do nothing with their beautiful pelts either.'

'You weren't workin' with me the other day, so listen to this,' Harry interrupted. 'At one the end of the paddock there was a mob of about thirty kangaroos and nearby was a flock of maybe three hundred head of sheep—and all were feedin' peaceful like.

'A small pack of five dingoes arrived, then easily climbed through the farmer's fence about fifty yards from where I was working. It's my bet the two largest were dad and mum and the smaller ones, their pups.

'Must've been downwind of 'em because they didn't appear to notice me.

'However, those dingoes obviously saw both the sheep and the roos, but amazingly they started stalking the roos, though there were many more sheep and lambs nearby that should have made much easier targets! Surely that behaviour must tell the local farmers something, eh? That's if they were prepared to listen.

'And do you know what Patrick? I've been thinking about this a lot lately. You only need to look around to see why it is that so many lambs die and that's because there's no protection for them from the elements during winter, which I've been told can be bloody harsh. That's *not* the fault of the dingoes, but they've become the scapegoats.

'Look, there might be good pasture everywhere, but the paddocks are otherwise as bare as a badger's bum. There's no shelter for the sheep... anywhere! I'd not be surprised if dingoes did take the odd sheep, but I reckon the real number of losses should be shafted back to the farmers: their animal husbandry is bloody woeful,' Harry emphasized as he angrily threw out the remnants of his mug of tea.

'Well put, agreed and understood,' replied Patrick. 'Regardless, I think it'd be futile for us to attempt to do anything about it. But if the silly buggers keep killing dingoes at the rate they do now, they'll eventually eradicate the whole damn lot... and that just *isn't right!*'

At the end of the day as the men were riding home, Patrick said sternly, 'Best not say too much about your views whenever we're at the pub, because one of their hideous poisons might find its way into your beer. I'm serious Harry, keep your wits about you and your trap shut.'

27

With approaching cold weather, Harry and Patrick agreed to retire all three of their ageing horses. They had all been faithful and often hardworking animals, not worthy of being put down when just beyond their prime; instead, they would be left to graze in peace on the old farm's lush pasture.

However, as luck would have it, not long after a neighbouring couple and their three young children called in to introduce themselves armed with a cake and two bottles of homemade ginger beer.

When conversation casually gravitated to polite interest in their horses, the children almost went berserk, begging their parents to buy them. 'Ooohh, come on Dad you've been promising us our own horses for years!'

'Hang on a few ticks, kids,' Harry intervened. 'What makes you think they're for sale? And how much money have you got?'

The eldest boy James, replied, 'only about twelve bob, but we'll work really, really hard on your place to earn the rest of what you want for them.'

'Ehhmm, now let me see,' Harry replied as if he was carefully mulling over the boy's offer. 'If you bring over your twelve bob, I reckon that should just about be enough. What do you reckon, Patrick?'

'Sounds like a fair enough deal to me, but you all must give your word that you will take good care of them. Do you reckon that agreement will be alright with your Mum and Dad?'

The gentle nod by their father and the smiles on both parent's faces completed the deal, as much as did the excited charge of the kids out the backdoor in search of their greatest ever gifts.

As Harry and Patrick walked with their neighbours to the front gate of the house yard, out of hearing range of the children of course, Patrick said, 'Harry was only joking about having your kids come over to work off their debt. Well, not if you'd prefer that they kept their word. There is no debt, my friends, we'll take their money, but we'll return it to you later without them knowing.'

Before either incredulous parent could say anything, Harry added, 'And you won't need to worry about buying saddles and bridles. Just please make sure your kids look after those animals.'

'Hang on a minute folks,' said Patrick sounding a note of alarm. It has just occurred to me that we'll need to keep our horses for another week or so, otherwise we won't be able to get about to buy our new horses. Do you reckon your kids can hold on and not be too disappointed?'

'Of course,' replied their mother. 'Leave it to me.'

* * *

THE TALK of money sparked some anxiety with Harry and Patrick. Until now they had been living comfortably off their wages, but to procure replacement horses they would now need more cash than they currently held.

The next day they rode into Scone armed with two small pouches containing enough gold they guessed would be sufficient to buy what they needed. They soon found the small Assayers Office, which fortunately was empty, except for the office manager.

'What can I do for you boys?' the manager asked politely. 'My name's Tom, Tom French.'

'We were wondering, Tom, can you turn our hard-earnt into cash?' Patrick asked with equal politeness. 'And quickly like because we need some money to buy a couple of decent remounts before someone else grabs 'em.'

'Of course, gentlemen, but you'll have to show me what you've got before I can answer that question.'

Harry and then Patrick, carefully emptied the contents of their pouches into separate, shiny weighing pans.

'Bloody hell gents, where did you get this lot?' Tom gasped.

'That, Tom, is for us to know, but for you to guess. We don't want prospectors crawling all over our find. But I can tell you it's about three days west from here,' Harry lied easily.

'Apologies gents. I didn't mean to pry but you have some high-quality metal here, that's certain enough. But you'll have to leave it with me until I've completed my assay. But don't worry, it *will be safe*; there's no bushrangers around here anymore and I run a trustworthy business. I'll give you separate receipts but the amounts I show cannot be exact.

'Return in two days' time and we can complete our transaction, providing I've got sufficient cash on hand. After that, your assets will be smelted and stamped with its purity and weight. The amount you receive in cash will not include my fees, of course.'

'Yes, of course, Tom, and it's so nice to know that there are no more bushrangers around to contend with, eh?' Patrick replied contentedly, but with a veiled threat.

Two days later, Harry and Patrick returned to the Assay Office. The settlement amount was much more than they expected.

However, just before dawn the following morning as Harry and Patrick were heading off to work, a lone rider charged past them, heading west.

'What a coincidence, eh Harry?' Patrick chuckled and said, 'Our assayer friend obviously took your bait.'

28

Scone was not short of quality horses... nor of rogues who cried poor when negotiating prices. However, after riding several horses and making their selections, Harry and Patrick felt vindicated that the asking prices were equine bargains: Walers, the owner called them. All were three years old, strong, responsive, highly intelligent, eager to work, companionable and above all else, easy to ride.

In Scone, before returning home the men not only purchased new saddles, halters, and bridles, but cold weather coats for each horse. They even lashed out and purchased a new saddlebag, agreeing that it was time to discard its predecessor, just in case someone ever recognised it.

On the way back to their farm, Harry and Patrick called in to collect the neighbour's children. They were overjoyed to be quickly seated on the men's new horses and then to be led in tow behind the old ones, back to Harry's and Patrick's farm.

As soon as they arrived, the children were in turn officially introduced to their mounts. After each child had been legged up into their saddle and the reins handed to them, much fuss was made by Harry and Patrick to make certain the stirrups were adjusted to suit each child. The children fidgeted, wanting desperately to get going.

'Just a sec young fella,' Harry asked somewhat sternly, albeit staged. 'You've got that twelve bob you owe us I suppose?'

'Yep, here you go, Harry,' said the youngest boy as he fumbled in his trouser pocket then handed over a fistful of coins. 'Don't worry, it's all there.'

Less than ten seconds later all three children were out the gate, laughing madly as they eagerly urged their newly acquired mounts into a canter while daring each other not to be last home.

* * *

FOR BOTH MEN it soon became a regular event to wave to the children as they proudly cantered their horses past their farmhouse; when they were either on the way to school, or when galloping by flat-out on some real or imagined adventure.

* * *

ON THE THIRD day of persistent rain, making it impossible to work outdoors, both men were totally bored and at wit's end. 'This is crazy Patrick,' Harry moaned. 'Being cooped up like this is nearly as bad as doing jail time.'

'I hope to never experience the difference, my friend,' replied Patrick. 'But you're right, grab your oil skins and hat, we need to present ourselves at one of the local pubs and do justice to a cold ale and perhaps a nice steak and eggs for lunch.'

When Harry and Patrick arrived at the nearest pub, they were impressed by its warmth, not just that generated by the open fire-place, but by the owner and the many patrons. In fact, the pub was crowded with many like-minded local folks, the majority men, carrying either an expanded girth, a bit of age, or both. And all seemed to have an opinion, about which several were shouting on top note that theirs was the only possible correct one.

Shortly after Patrick and Harry had finished their lunches, the voices became louder and the promise of a fight erupted. Chairs were hastily dragged across the floor and a table thrown aside to clear a space to enable the two antagonists to engage. 'Harry, sit!' Patrick ordered as he placed a vicelike grip onto one of his friend's arms. 'This stoush is none of our business, but there's no reason not to watch on. Could be good entertainment, eh?'

However, before a blow was thrown, Jimbo the pub keeper, a sizable gent armed with a short black club, leapt over the bar counter. He quickly pushed his way into the middle of the ring formed by his patrons, then planted himself firmly between the assailants.

Up close, and staring face to face with the largest of them, Jimbo yelled. 'Now listen to me, Hugh. I've told you theivin' bastards to keep out of my pub, so get out before I throw you out!'

In a blur of movement Hugh reacted, cocking his right arm perhaps thinking that a quick punch to Jimbo's face would allow the fight to continue without further interference. But that was wishful thinking because Jimbo reacted even faster, slashing his club down the side of Hugh's face, cleanly shaving off his ear.

Hugh screamed in pain and clutched in astonishment at the side of his head where his ear had once been. 'Agghh, Jimbo. Why'd yah do that? Look what you've done yah bastard! By the jeezes Jimbo, look at all me blood. What if I bleed tah death!?'

'Your problem entirely,' Jimbo replied dispassionately as he reached down and pulled Hugh to his feet. Not missing a beat, Jimbo dragged Hugh by the neck of his scruffy jacket to a side door. Despite Hugh's whimpering and while still clutching his mutilated ear, Jimbo firmly booted Hugh outside and into the rain.

As Jimbo walked triumphantly back to behind the bar, Patrick started a slow hand clap. Harry quickly followed, reinforcing the beat. Within seconds the entire patronage was clapping, but laughter and cheers soon replaced the clapping.

When the excitement ebbed and some normality returned to the pub's dining room, Patrick learnt from one of the men sitting at an adjoining table that Hugh was a well-known, though luckless bushranger who was thought to have once ridden with the far more famous, though deceased master bushranger, Captain Thunderbolt.

'Well Harry, I guess that's our entertainment for today; we'd better make tracks for home. Thinking about it and looking around, every bloke here resembles a god- damn bushranger.'

'Including us?' Harry asked with a grin.

'Yep, it takes one to know one, eh?'

* * *

THE RAIN STOPPED by the time they were home. Harry then lamented wearily, 'Yah know what Patrick? I didn't see one good-looking woman all day; in fact, I don't recall seeing any women.'

'Well I did,' Patrick replied mischievously. 'It so happens that Jimbo's assistant is not his sister, and a comely lady indeed. And, my good friend, she had no objection to my suggestion that we meet again soon. In fact, it was her suggestion that we can meet at any time... and preferably not at the pub.'

'You really are a sly bugger,' Harry replied. 'I suppose that you'll soon want me to move out, so that she can move in?'

'Don't be getting too hasty Harry. I only met the fair lass two hours ago! By the way, her name is Patricia. How about that... Patrick and Patricia; Pat for short. Got a nice ring to it, eh.'

29

That night as the men relaxed in the warmth radiating from their lounge room fireplace, Patrick said, 'Well go on, what's on your mind? You haven't spoken for more than an hour. It's not Pat, I hope.'

'Nah, you know what you're doing, Harry replied. 'However, can I ask you a few personal questions?'

'Of course, but I ask you to respect what I tell you and never repeat to anyone, anything that I say.'

'Fair enough. So before we met did you ever marry?'

'Twice, if you really must know. The first lasted only a few months. She wanted to live in Scotland; I didn't. She wanted children; I didn't. We parted amicably enough, but I never heard from her again, nor did I pursue her.'

'And the second?'

'Well, she was a beauty, educated and intelligent. That marriage lasted nearly six years. Most of it a man could not have wished for better. I worked my backside off for her, reworking the fences on her small property and re-modelling her cottage... to suit *her* needs only as it transpired.

'She obviously had plans in mind that didn't include me, and it didn't sit well with me that she chose to invent stories implying I was somehow a *lay about* and *always betraying her*. Nonsensical stuff and utter rubbish of course.

'However, I eventually walked out on her, leaving her nothing... and no kids: thank God. Anyway, that's when I joined the British Navy and worked my way up through the ranks.

'Thereafter, well, far better that I then had a girl in every port.

'Any more questions, my inquisitive friend?'

'Not really, though you don't seem to be a particularly good judge of female company.'

'Touché, Harry. So when pray tell, are *you* intending to surrender yourself to the intimacies of a beautiful woman's body?'

'All in good time, as you would say; all in good time. Mind you, in the meantime, I still live in hope.'

* * *

OVER THE NEXT few weeks Patrick seemed to Harry to have changed his persona completely. He was seldom up before mid-morning and appeared exhausted when he did rise. Though he wasn't either argumentative or grumpy, he just seemed disinterested in most things Harry talked about, though he did maintain regular ablutions and kept his beard well-trimmed.

Patrick also lost interest in his off-farm job and it wasn't long after that he realised his previous readily available cash had taken a major hit. *'Can you lend me a few quid Harry? I'll square things with you next week. C'mon, there's a good lad,'* became all too frequent and unwelcome conversation.

To Patrick's annoyance, Harry's charity soon ceased. 'Well, bugger you, Harry,' Patrick yelled over his shoulder as he stormed out of the cottage, slamming the door behind him. 'I'll do without your damn money.'

At about three o'clock the following morning, Harry was rudely awakened by a very dishevelled and agitated Patrick. There was no mistaking the look of urgency on his friend's face, nor the desperate tone in his voice.

'Harry! Harry! You have to get up man, and quickly!'

'Alright, alright, I'm awake. What the hell's going on? Have you just murdered somebody?'

'No, no. Not that; worse! I've just burnt down a hay shed and a church! C'mon, get dressed, we need to scarper before daylight.'

'Why on earth would you want to burn down a hay shed and a church in the middle of the night?' Harry asked pragmatically, trying to defuse some of Patrick's anxiety while guiding him to a chair in their lounge room.

'Now, sit! Just lean back Patrick and take a few deep breaths for God's sake... and *try* to relax!

'There, that seems better. Had you been drinking or what?'

'No, no... well, yes actually. I'd had a few rums earlier on.'

'So, you were no doubt drunk? Why, pray tell and were you with anyone?'

After a few seconds of reflection, Patrick appeared to have calmed himself, but nevertheless he was obviously keen to unburden himself. 'Mate, it was all an overreaction on one part and unfortunate clumsiness by the other part.

'You see, Pat had been nibbling my neck. Yes, I'd had a few grogs, but she seemed determined to retire to the privacy of the hayshed where we usually... you know...?'

'Yeah, I can guess. Go on.'

'Well, when we got inside, there was already a dim light glowing in between some stacked sheaves of hay. All looked most cosy I must say. And there were familiar mumblings of the most erotic type coming from behind those sheaves. My natural curiosity took over and I soon discovered who had the audacity to be using our hay shed. You'll never guess who it was.'

'No probably not but get on with it.'

'The vicar and one of his younger parishioners, no less.'

'And...?'

'Totally ignoring their obvious hard-earned arousal, both panicked when they realised they had an audience.

'She unfairly cursed me in a most unladylike manner, shoved the vicar off, then grabbed their fuel lamp and threw it straight at me, only just missing I must add.

'But, before we could exchange names and pleasantries, *whooof*, up went the hay sheaves: it was bloody amazing how quickly the flames shot up and almost to the roof in just a few seconds!

'Anyway, I grabbed Pat, towed her out the shed's door and then we sprinted down the path that leads beside the church. Now this, Harry, is where responsibility becomes really blurred. Yes, I was still carrying our fuel lamp and I did drop the bloody thing when I tripped over someone's cat. But surely, I can't be responsible for the church having been built right there, can I? So you see, suddenly flames were also now shooting up the church's side wall and I was not going to hang around and volunteer to put out either of those God-damn fires!

'And Harry, I'm bloody certain that nobody will believe my story over that which the most trusted vicar could concoct in *his* defence.'

'Alright Patrick, alright. But is there anything else you need to tell me?'

'Yes, as a matter of fact there is.

'I never thought I'd ever see a vicar in the buff and in such a phys-ical predicament as he was.

'And after I'd cleared the town, I discovered that Pat had somehow nicked my money-belt which, as you've no doubt already predicted, held most of *your* unspent funds: that no good, thieving whore!

'However, more to the point Harry, do we now scarper, or not?'

'Yep, we scarper. I'll bring the horses in and get 'em saddled. You'd best start packing and when you've finished, get rid of your beard.'

* * *

As THE FALSE dawn faded and the first light of day splashed across the tree canopies and paddocks, Harry and Patrick, now both beardless, stopped to rest beside a small babbling brook at least five miles south of Scone.

None of their three horses were labouring and there had been no traffic whatsoever. Regardless, to avoid being seen, they chose to bypass every future settlement.

At noon they stopped again to rest and further consider their options.

30

Even though the chances of them being recognised were minuscule, only now that they were more than one hundred and fifty miles from Scone, would Harry and Patrick seek overnight accommodation; and that only ensued when the weather turned cold, or particularly windy, or both.

Their Walers performed magnificently during the following month. All three horses seemed undaunted by the challenges of ever-changing landscapes and routinely gave easily recognisable head-shakes warning Harry and Patrick long before approaching travellers came into sight... and thereby allowing them timely retreats into the safety of roadside scrub.

Their luck held; most travellers showed scant regard to them. Most however, acknowledged them with either a friendly wave, a smile or head nod. A few stopped to have a chat. Of identity recognition, there was none.

Not only had the vast plains country become more heavily wooded, but they learnt that a massive river called the Murray awaited their arrival about three days riding further south.

'That should do us nicely, Harry, my boy. Perhaps you'll give me consent to teach you how to swim properly, eh?'

* * *

Neither man was disappointed when they first sighted the Murray River. From its bank, high above the water line, they gazed in awe upon the river.

'We won't be getting across here any time soon my good friend; she's gotta be at least a hundred and fifty yards wide,' Patrick estimated and quickly added, with just a tinge of ribbing, 'and you haven't yet benefitted from my swimming tutelage.'

At first glance, the river was just a flat, shimmering expanse that disappeared in both directions. But as they stared in wonder, they could almost feel its might as it relentlessly shouldered a pathway to some far-off destination. And they were fascinated by the many powerful upsurges and swirls, the offspring of continuous conflict between submerged obstructions daring to challenge the river's power.

The dry air not only carried a strong eucalypt fragrance but was filled with the monotonous buzzing of countless unknown insects. The bird life too, was prolific: sulphur crested cockatoos, grey and pink Major Mitchell parrots and many other smaller, gaudy parrots —either "talking" to each other or screeching in mock alarm at the men's intrusion.

Wild ducks and at least five other different aquatic bird species were everywhere, the most prominent being huge white pelicans.

The day was at its hottest as the men strolled contentedly through the dappled shade cast by the ancient and massive redgums surrounding them. Some of those giants which once lined the river's banks had been undermined long ago and now lay partly submerged. To Harry's and Patrick's delight they noticed several tortoises sunbaking on the trunks of those trees, just above the water line. But as they approached to get a better look at the strange plate-like creatures, they would unexpectedly dive back into the river, their rapid decent following the shafts of the ever-diffusing golden sunbeams that also sought the river's depths.

'Well I vote that we camp here for a while; what say you, Harry?'

'The same!' Harry replied eagerly. 'It's a bloody beautiful spot. But you'd better move your left foot before that tiger snake you damn near trod on bites yah!

'And mate, for Heaven's sake, what's with yah strange walk and why are yah scratchin' yourself all the time?'

'The dreaded pox I suspect, Harry. And yes, it's getting worse every day. I'll definitely need the services of a doctor in the very near future.'

* * *

FIRST THING THE FOLLOWING MORNING, Harry said as he made no attempt to stifle a yawn, 'Did you hear cattle during the night?'

'I did. Woke me up, too. From my limited experience I'd say it's most unusual to be mustering cattle in the dead of night.'

'I'm thinking cattle duffers,' Harry suggested seriously. 'So what do yah say we have some breakfast, then go looking for them cattle? I'll take the shotgun just in case; I might get a shot at some ducks.'

About four hundred yards downstream from their camp, they came upon the tracks of at least a dozen cattle and two horses. On a straight section of the river, fresh tracks led down the riverbank, then stopped at the water line.

Just as Harry and Patrick scanned the far bank, two horsemen appeared from the timber and without slowing, urged their mounts down the opposite bank and started across the river to where Harry and Patrick sat motionless on their horses.

'They haven't seen us yet, Harry, but you'd best nurse your shotgun just in case they can't contain their surprise when they arrive. I'm assuming of course that you've got it loaded?'

As both approaching horses scrambled to the top of the near riverbank, they brutally reined in their horses as they spotted Harry and Patrick calmly watching them.

'Nice morning for a swim, boys,' said Patrick in a tone laced with sarcasm.

'Had no trouble getting your cattle over, I assume? You'd be well advised not to go for your firearms. Mind you, ours is only a single barrel shotgun, but my friend here is a wonderful shot. In fact, I've never seen him miss anything he's ever aimed at. And rest assured if either one of you wants to chance your luck, which one of you really wants to die on such a beautiful morning as this? No takers? Well just in case, kindly throw down your weapons; all of them! Now!'

'Ride slowly in front of us if you please, gentlemen, and show a bit of respect to your horses,' Harry ordered somewhat cynically, then added in a more sociable tone, 'we'd just like to have a peaceful chat back at our camp and when we've finished, you can be off to do whatever you had planned. Behave yourselves and you'll both get your weapons back... but only *if* you behave! Is that understood, boys?'

Back at the camp, Patrick ordered, most matter-of-factly, that both stranger's dismount, then added, 'Take a seat on that log, lads, and introduce yourselves properly to Harry while I make us all a nice cup of tea. You'll have to help yourself if you want sugar.

'Right, now we're all comfortable I'm assuming that Bluey and Manfred are in fact your real names. I'm Patrick. We aren't interested in whatever it was that you were up to last night, we just need information such as where we can safely cross the river, where's the nearest town with a proper doctor and whether or not we should be on the lookout for unfriendly bushrangers; not including your good selves, of course. And nothing will be said about our little chat, agreed?'

'Yeah, righto,' said Bluey, sounding relaxed, 'they're our real names, but no surnames, eh?'

'Understood, but please, go on Bluey,' Patrick urged.

'Well, at this time of year, you can easily ford the river where you sprung us just now. There're other places upstream and downstream from here, but you need to know the signs before getting your feet wet, like, for instance, where the sandbars and submerged tree trunks are located.

'As far as a doctor's concerned, you'd not do any better than the lady doctor in Albury. She's getting on a bit but has certain sympathies and understandings which have been known to provide comfort to the odd bushranger. Even that bastard, Morgan!

'Anyway, her name's Margaret. Dunno her surname, but you'll be able to contact her at the hospital I reckon.'

'And that stupid shit, Morgan, he's still in this region,' Manfred chimed in. 'The traps refer to him as Mad Dog Morgan.'

'Sounds like he's to be avoided,' said Harry. 'Does Morgan operate alone or with a gang?'

'He's had many blokes working with him over the years,' Bluey continued, 'but since he shot and killed a few local coppers, there's like only two or three still ridin' with him. Well, that's the last we heard anyway.'

Without any prompting, Manfred then changed the subject. 'If yah need to get into Albury, real soon like, then there's a paddle steamer that should arrive tomorrow at a turnaround point about five miles downstream from here.'

Harry and Patrick immediately looked at each other in surprise. That'll do us quite nicely,' Patrick replied. 'Thanks Manfred, but who would look after our horses?'

'No trouble,' said Bluey, 'if you both give the skipper a hand loading wood for his boilers, he'll probably find a place for them on board. If he does, just slip him a few bob when you arrive at Albury.

'Best tell him first, though, that Bluey and Manfred recommended you. So now, can we be making tracks?'

'Fair enough lads; we appreciate your advice,' replied Patrick. 'Yes, of course. Grab your firearms and be on your way, and good luck, eh?'

'Not so rough on your horses, eh fellas,' Harry reminded their visitors as they left the camp site and headed north.

31

'Ehhmm, not the worst case I've ever seen, but bad enough,' Doctor Margaret replied in response to Patrick's request for a prognosis of his itch. 'You'll live but, bad luck, as you put it, has nothing to do with the facts of life, sir. Can you give me the name of your lady friend, after all she needs treatment just as urgently as you do?

'If you can do that, despite what you might think of her, you could be saving her life. She'll receive my private note along with the medications I send her, advising how to properly use everything.'

'I'll give you fifty quid for the medication, but what surety can you give me that it will all be delivered?'

'Sir, I can only give you my word that I'll do my best. But I'm a doctor, not a postal delivery service. Regardless, your gesture is appreciated and will probably be most timely. Be assured, your name will not be revealed or implied *by me*. Let her guess.'

'Thank you, Margaret. Sorry, *Doctor*. But how do *I* get rid of this infernal itch?'

'Most importantly, sir, refrain from any further sexual shenanigans until the itch clears up... completely. Then burn all your current underwear and purchase several new items. Wear them once only before immediately washing them. And only wash them in boiling water.

'Even more importantly, see that you bathe *at least every other day*. Commit yourself now, to applying and taking the medications I've prepared, *every day!*'

'Or?'

'*Do nothing and die an unnecessary and lingering death over the next few months!*

'Now sir, take my salves and potions and please be on your way. Your fifty quid will *just* cover everything, so don't expect any change.'

* * *

WHEN PATRICK EMERGED from his consultation, Harry was there to greet him with the news that he had found suitable accommodation overlooking the river on the outskirts of Albury. 'The only problem I've found is that there's a bloody snake in the woodheap,' advised Harry, 'so watch out for it, eh.'

After unpacking and then turning out their horses to the side paddock, Harry lit the kitchen stove to make them a well-deserved cuppa. 'So, come on, out with it, Patrick... the verdict, that is. What did your lady doctor have to say?'

'Only if you promise not to laugh, because it's no laughing matter.'

'Yeah, yeah, alright, but leave nothing out!'

As Patrick's description approached its conclusion, the smallest of smiles flickered across Harry's face and a chuckle gently shook his chest.

Patrick's mistake was that he decided to pause from his somewhat embellished storytelling after he noticed Harry's red face and watering eyes. Instantly, Harry lost his now fragile self-control and burst into laughter, slapping his hands on his knees.

Patrick immediately joined him; both then roaring like demented lunatics, all the while wiping away tears of their misplaced joy.

A semblance of control only occurred when Harry, overcome and gasping for breath, ran outside to avoid looking at Patrick's ongoing contortions.

* * *

THE NEXT MORNING, Harry, and Patrick rode into Albury. Harry went to exchange more gold for cash and for Patrick to buy several pairs of men's undergarments, blocks of soap and new towels.

It was while they stopped for lunch at a pub that they overheard about the early arrival of a paddle steamer. 'Yeah, the paddle steamer's Captain and his crew loaded the wood they needed at the normal pick-up point about four miles downstream and deposited payment in the usual place, as usual like,' an old chap explained loudly and excitedly to his mate, 'but apparently, just as she were about to round the first bend comin' *thisa way*, Morgan just rode up all casual like and nicked all the money belong'n to the timber cutters!

'The cutters blamed the skipper apparently. The five of em' rode into town to dob the skipper into the cops... for tellin' Morgan about their payment system.

'Anyway, I'm told the skipper and his crew 'ave sorted everythin'. Skipper even paid 'em a second time, in good faith like, but the cops refused to give the cutters' a free hand to go after Morgan. Said they'd take care of everything.'

'Yeah, right, I'd like to see that,' the old man's friend replied sceptically.

32

———————

Late that afternoon, prompted by Patrick's suggestion that duck would be nice on the evening menu, Harry took his shotgun and a few cartridges and soon disappeared behind the wall of red gum eucalypts which reached to the shoulders of both banks of the river.

As Harry quickly discovered, there was no shortage of ducks. His meanderings sent many of them whirring into the air ahead of him. 'On the next rise, I'll be ready for you little buggers,' he murmured.

Seconds later, a pair of plump wood ducks launched, scarpering at full speed toward a billabong on his left. In one smooth movement, Harry brought the butt of the shotgun to his shoulder. Sweeping the barrel to his left but keeping it just in advance of the ducks' line of flight, he fired. Feathers flew. With soft thuds, both ducks crashed onto the hard-baked earth, sending up small puffs of dust before coming to an undignified stop.

Harry expertly broke the breech of his shotgun, but the spent cartridge shell failed to eject. Rather than swear at this inconvenience, he simply rummaged around in his trouser pocket until he found what he was after. 'Ah, there you are my beauty. Do your magic, baby,' Harry muttered as he dropped his tiny pocketknife down the end of the still smoking gun's barrel.

Having no further use for the spent cartridge, he threw it as far as he could into the river. He watched mesmerised as it bobbed to the surface and was then swept swiftly along until it finally submerged, a hundred or so yards downstream. After carefully returning the knife to his pocket, he collected his kills and returned to camp.

Both men thoroughly enjoyed their roasted ducks, judging by the amount of gravy smeared on their cheeks and saturating their beards.

Later, while enjoying their final cup of tea for the evening, a thoughtful Patrick said, 'I think it'd be interesting to meet those timber cutters; they sound like enterprising lads. If they aren't up for a chat, then perhaps we could do a bit of fishing on the way back.'

'Yeah, I'll be in that,' replied Harry, 'but you realise we don't have any fishing tackle or bait of any kind? Mind you, I reckon we can buy bait in town, or dig for worms. Knowing your luck lately, Patrick, you'll probably find gold... yeah, fool's gold.'

'Very funny Harry.'

* * *

HAVING PURCHASED some basic fishing tackle and regardless of their disappointment to locate many worms of "hook size," they nonetheless went in search of the wood cutters' camp.

Generally they followed the riverbank, but where the trees and undergrowth proved impenetrable they were forced to head away from the river to navigate their way downstream. Just as they were about to exit one particularly dense stand of undergrowth, Harry's horse, which was leading, stopped dead, threw up its head and whinnied a familiar, barely audible warning.

Two things were obvious as Patrick nudged his horse forward to be beside Harry. First, their chosen path forward was blocked by a river backwater and second, about one hundred yards away, three riders were disappearing at a fair clip, weaving their way between the trunks of the river red gums.

'Do you reckon they've seen us, Patrick?'

'Oh yes, but they know they're in no danger; we can't follow them, even if we wanted to. I suggest we just ignore them.'

By early afternoon they stumbled upon the wood cutters' camp. Albeit with some suspicion, five men, all who appeared to be in their early thirties to forties, stood up from their log chairs to greet Harry and Patrick.

'G'day; got time for a chat?' Patrick asked jovially. 'We'd like to know if you can show us where we can dig for some decent sized worms.'

Harry then quickly added. 'And we could do with a cuppa if you've got one on the go. Don't worry, we've got our own makin's.'

It wasn't long, after introductions all round, that the five wood cutters were comfortably exchanging snippets of their former lives and talking about their ambitions. All had wives and children and were desperately trying to get some money together so they could spoil their wives and ensure their children would get an education... which inevitably led to them expressing their opinions on all bushrangers; of one in particular, Mad Dan Morgan.

'So, you've actually met him, face to face?' Harry asked in an innocent tone. 'What's he like?'

'Yeah, more than once; he's a right bastard alright,' Nathaniel the oldest cutter, replied, obviously keen to expand on his experiences. 'These days, only two blokes tag along with him. They seem to stay in the background. But Morgan, for such a small chap, has an enormous chip on his shoulder and an overblown belief that he's... what's the word; ah yeah, *invincible*.

'Here mate, read this, it'll tell you all you need to know,' said Nathaniel as he handed an old newspaper clipping to Patrick. 'Apparently he's already shot three coppers dead.'

The article read:

The "most bloodthirsty ruffian that ever took to the bush in Australia", and "one of the most determined and bloodthirsty of colonial freebooters".

'The bastard just bobs up anywhere,' Nathaniel continued. 'He'll pretend friendliness and good humour one minute and the next minute he'll be holding a god-damn gun under yah nose.

'Just like the other day. Met us out where we were work'n. We got talk'n then *wham* out comes his handgun and he tells his two mates to hold us there while he relieves us of our pay. Seems he just wants to rob everyone blind, like.

'So keep a sharp lookout for them bastards. If Morgan takes a liking to your horses, he'll try to relieve you of them too; don't you worry about that!

'Oh yeah. By the way, there's one thing he hates. Can't stand bein' called *Daniel*, even though that's his middle name. He's OK with *Mad Dan* mind you, but gets all antsy like when anyone calls him Daniel.'

'Points well taken, mate,' Harry interrupted gently. 'It was good of the skipper to reimburse you fellas. He's on your side, as we are.

'But c'mon, where can we get some bait?'

'Come with me,' said Sandy, clearly the youngest member of the work team.

* * *

FOR AN HOUR OR SO SANDY, Harry and Patrick wandered about under the huge red gums looking for the tell-tale signs of an underground grub, which according to local indigenous folk, were the number one bait for fish, in particular the huge Murray cod.

As soon as a suitable sized hole was located, Sandy went to work. Using a length of small gauge fencing wire which he had fashioned so that one end resembled a corkscrew and the other end a small crank handle, he carefully inserted his "gotcha tool" into the hole. If he felt a *softish* resistance, he'd slowly rotate the wire three or so turns then carefully withdraw the wire. If they were lucky, Sandy would withdraw a fat, squirming, whitish-brown grub about four inches long, firmly held in the corkscrew.

'Not just good bait,' Sandy said, 'but according to the Blacks, good eating too. I've tried 'em, cooked like; not too bad, but I'd rather eat cod.'

* * *

HARRY AND PATRICK RODE about a mile further downstream from the wood cutters' camp, then reined in when they found what Sandy had described as the perfect cod hole; a partially submerged confusion of the denuded trunks and branches from two ancient gums and over-hanging branches of live trees.

Harry was the first to get snagged, but a few minutes later Patrick announced that apparently, he too, was in the same predicament. But not so.

Suddenly the line in Patrick's hand raced away. Slightly panicked, he gripped the line, hard. He then yelled in pain, instantly dropping the line, which continued to snake towards the sunken tree trunks. In disbelief he inspected his hand, not expecting to see much but was astonished to realise that the burn he'd received was not only sting-ing, but bleeding.

'Shit and buggery!' he swore, loud enough for Harry to hear, then looked up to see if Harry *had* heard him.

Realising his friend was in some sort of trouble, Harry ceased his futile attempt to unsnag his own line and jogged over to Patrick.

'I've seen worse, yah big sook. Here, give me your line, I'll show you how it's done.'

Though Harry cleverly fought the fish, he soon found himself scrambling to avoid being pulled into the river. Gradually the fish tired, but did not surrender, at least not without its own final, unsuc-cessful, but equally gallant attempt to gain refuge amongst the submerged branches.

Eventually they beached the fish. 'Bloody hell! Harry exclaimed,' what do you reckon it weighs?'

'About twenty pounds I reckon,' came a calm, but unfamiliar voice from the top of the riverbank. 'Can you both manage, or can I give you a hand up?'

'That sounds rather gracious of you Daniel, but first let me dispatch our catch,' replied Patrick as he frowned and winked at Harry, hoping he'd understand his warning.

'But then again, Daniel, we'll manage,' Patrick taunted, 'you surely don't want to get *my* blood on your grubby hands as well.'

33

Harry and Patrick scrambled up the riverbank, carrying their catch and fishing tackle. Totally ignoring Morgan and his men, they walked to Harry's horse and started repacking their saddlebags, Patrick on the near side closest to Morgan, while Harry casually walked to the far side of his mount.

Patrick removed the newspaper lining his side of the saddle bag and passed it across the horse's rump to Harry, suggesting that he wrap their fish in it to keep the flies away. While Patrick placed their fishing tackle and remaining bait into his side of the saddlebag, Harry made a fuss of carefully wrapping their catch. Patrick slowly turned to face Morgan, then rested against the flank of Harry's horse.

'So who the hell are you two and what was that smart-arse remark all about; about blood being on my hands?' Morgan demanded, his voice now loud, there being no pretence that his frustration was on the rise, attempting to stamp his authority.

'There's no use denying it, it's well known you're a murdering imbecile who shoots coppers in cold blood. Three now isn't it, Daniel? But you won't be adding *my* blood to your tally.'

'By the jeezus, I can fix that for you right now, you mealy mouthed bastard!' Morgan yelled. But alas, given his high state of agitation and accelerating temper, he only managed to fumble... and then drop his handgun!

Ignominious chuckles ensued from mad Dog's cohorts, further exacerbating his rage as he readied himself to dive for his gun.

'I'd leave it right there if I were you, Daniel,' Patrick warned quickly, 'you see, Harry there, he never misses. Does he boys?'

Addle-brained and now totally confused, Morgan spun to see that Harry had emerged from behind his horse. It wasn't the shock of seeing Harry which made him gasp audibly, but to now be staring down the barrel of a shotgun, unwaveringly pointing at his chest, certainly had.

It only took Morgan just seconds to react. Spinning to face his companions, he yelled, 'well go on, shoot these bastards; he's the only one with a gun and there's two of you!' Go on, shoot the bastards, or so help me I'll...'

'Or you'll do what?' Harry asked, recognising the look of despair and desperation that now clouded Morgan's face.

'What the hell's goin' on here?' Morgan screamed, 'I pay you two to cover my back. You owe me!'

'Not anymore,' Manfred responded, 'You're an idiot, Morgan. You're not as smart as you think; Patrick here had you so wound up that you never realised he was distracting you while Harry was getting his shotgun.'

'Besides, we've met these blokes,' Bluey added, 'and guess what? They're not bad to the bone like you!'

Completely ignoring Morgan, Harry walked over to shake the hands of both onlookers. 'How yah keeping Bluey; you too Manfred?' Harry asked, 'I still dunno why on earth you two want anything to do with this dolt. Here, hang onto his lordship's handgun, he's not going to need it where he's going.'

'It's the usual thing, Harry, money, or rather, the lack of it. We're both broke.'

'Yeah, they're also both useless,' Morgan muttered. 'No guts, that's their problem.'

'We don't think so,' Manfred replied. 'You're nothing but a

deranged idiot. I hope your mother loved you because we certainly don't. Which reminds me, you still haven't squared us for that wood cutters' job.'

'Oh yes,' quipped Patrick, 'I'll bet you haven't had a chance to spend any of it, so cough it up, Daniel; give it to me. Now! I'm going to divide it two ways, for Bluey and Manfred. That's right, Daniel, you get none! Now, if you would please, Bluey and Manfred, tie him up with this; around his ankles too if you would.'

A few minutes later, Bluey asked, 'You took a bit of a risk, Patrick, bad mouthin' him and not knowing that we were with this idiot, when you was down the riverbank, fishin', like.'

'True, but not a big risk. I knew Morgan's features well enough. The wood cutters described him to a tee. I figured that he would have his eye on relieving us of our horses, having spotted us as we made our way to the cutters camp. That's when I first thought I sighted you lot, though I wasn't certain it *was* you. And you also followed us later when we went fishing.

'You followed us of course because Morgan thought we *hadn't seen you*!

'However, we hid in the scrub near that backwater and we both recognised you two with Morgan as you rode past us. And knowing you two from our earlier meeting, I reckoned we could trust you to stay neutral, or lend us a hand before he had a chance to act. Don't worry, I had explained my plan to Harry long before introducing ourselves to Morgan.'

'Right, so what are you going to do with this stupid arse?' Manfred asked.

'I'm going to give him a choice. Are you listening carefully, Daniel?' Patrick replied in a tone that would give inspiration to any traveling court judge.

'First, how about we leave him tied up and then *accidentally* throw him into the river? He'd drown of course. Or perhaps he'd appreciate it if we took him back to the wood cutters' camp and get him to apologise for inconveniencing them... and then leave him with those five annoyed and very strong wood cutter lads to see that he gets the thrashing of his life. Or, or just maybe, he could stay here. Of course, we four could give him a decent bit of tap. Just what's needed; a near death anaesthetic before one of you boys remove both of the bastard's trigger fingers. Then we leave him here alone, to bleed to death.'

'I say we get all the boys together and take a vote,' said Bluey, 'but what the bastard really deserves is the full throat of Harry's shotgun!' Or, mind you, we could just hand him in to the cops and collect a substantial reward.

* * *

THAT NIGHT, just as Harry and Patrick finished their second serve of succulent, grilled Murray cod, Patrick casually remarked, 'Do you think Mad Dog will bleed out?'

'Don't give a damn, actually,' Harry said, stifling a yawn. 'But you really are a cunning fella, Patrick.'

'Not really, my friend. Anyone can cast a sprat to catch a mackerel.

'Besides, there was no way he was ever getting his thieving grubby hands on *our* horses, eh?'

* * *

THE FOLLOWING DAY, Patrick rode into Albury and quite by coincidence met

the paddle-steamer skipper who had been "bothered" by Mad Dog. 'Your luck's in, mate. It so happens I've got something here for you; from two of Morgan's now defunct gang,' said Patrick, sounding quite pleased with himself as he handed over a wad of cash.

'I won't ask how you came by this money, but it's most welcome. But did you know I've already reimbursed those wood cutters; had to, or otherwise I'd have gone out of business.'

'"Fair's fair" they said, so you're all square then?'

'Yep, and I am grateful. But since then I've lost me deck hand and both of me furnace feeders. I've got goods and passengers that need to get moving, but I can't do everything on my own.'

141

'I just happen to know a couple of strong chaps who are looking for work; I'll send them in to you.'

Two days later, as a paddle steamer nudged past Harry's and Patrick's small riverside abode, the skipper sounded four long blasts on the boat's steam horn, to hopefully attract attention. It did. Seconds later, Harry burst from the back door, with Patrick only a step behind.

Once outside they soon saw three men waving like loons towards them from the boat's steering cabin roof; the skipper, and on either side of him were Bluey and Manfred.

34

ABOUT SIX MONTHS LATER

'I say Harry, I can now confidently announce I've rid myself of that infernal itch.'

'Glad to hear it; I'm sick of seeing you dancing about in your saddle as if you're sitting on a nest of jack jumpers.'

'Which reminds me, Harry, I've been talking with a few blokes down at the pub. They reckon they've come all the way from Adelaide on a paddle steamer. How about that? Keen hunters apparently. Somehow, they've learnt there are wild pigs in the country northwest of the Murray and seem hell-bent on potting a few. Apparently not far from here. Fancy your chances?'

'Getting bored, eh? Well, me too. I could do with a decent ride and our nags are putting on too much weight. Anyway, I wonder what that country up there looks like? When do you want to take off?'

'How about tomorrow? No fanfare of course.'

'But Harry, there's something else that's been nagging at me. Just a feeling; that's all, nothing else. I haven't been able to put my finger on it, until I read the latest newspaper at the pub. Just a few sentences that caught my eye.

'It seems the New South Wales police may have just stumbled upon a theory that there were other contenders in the Copeland gold theft. They've appointed some young hot-shot detective to reinvestigate everything and apparently, he's right on the tail of a couple of suspects.'

'Oh, shiiiit!' Harry replied angrily, 'That's bloody marvellous, eh? We've made a mistake somewhere along the way, or we've been far too bloody complacent, haven't we? So what do you suggest we do?'

'First, we again remove our beards. I think I'll shave off my hair completely as well; go bald, like. Why don't you grow a moustache, it can only improve your looks while making you look just a bit different?'

'And then, well, I doubt that our investigator chap will have any jurisdiction in Victoria, so as soon as we finish our little foray into pig country, we then head south into Victoria and stay there, well out of harm's way.'

* * *

AFTER FORDING THE MURRAY RIVER, downstream near a small settlement named Howlong, Harry and Patrick steadily headed northwest. Though the red gum eucalypt trees dominated for several miles, the terrain gradually gave way to an undulating, open landscape.

An occasional billabong provided fresh water, lush feed for their horses and shade when the noon temperature started to soar. All this not only sheltered many bird types and reptiles, but hordes of bloodthirsty mosquitoes. At their latest discovery they not only found signs of cattle... but finally, signs of pigs galore.

Rather than stay at this location that night, they camped about three hundred yards away, their theory being their presence at the water hole would alarm any pigs, leaving no targets for Harry in the morning.

They were right, for when Harry and Patrick emerged from their sleeping bags, there were several small herds noisily foraging on the open land, albeit all close to the billabong.

Keeping low, even crawling at times to stay hidden as best he could, Harry moved toward the nearest herd. As luck would have it, he was downwind.

Judging his distance to be no more than forty yards from the nearest pig, he slowly rose to his knees, brought the butt of his shotgun to his shoulder... and fired. Harry knew immediately that he had a clean kill but was amazed at how quickly—and noisily—the many nearby pigs charged away, squealing on top note, most heading for the thick scrub surrounding the waterhole. The balance headed for open ground and then disappeared over a small rise.

To relieve his aching legs and back, Harry stood slowly, expecting to see Patrick riding up to join him.

However, to his enormous and never to be forgotten surprise, he was confronted by four naked and highly agitated black men. They were all now rattling their throwing sticks against some very long spears indeed... then unexpectedly started shouting tirades which Harry interpreted as confrontational threats and abuse.

But then the penny dropped. Harry placed his gun on the ground, picked up his kill, then walked toward the black men. When almost upon them and well within range of their deadly, still rattling spears, he placed the pig back onto the ground and walked away, his unprotected back on full display to the blacks.

The rattling and abuse stopped. However, one individual, perhaps the small mob's leader, walked up to Harry, stopped barely eighteen inches away, then, not so gently pushed his hand into Harry's back.

'Easy now Harry, he just wants us to piss-off, I'd reckon. I think you just nicked their tucker,' called Patrick as he walked slowly, unarmed, towards the potential adversaries.

'Just smile and point to him, then at the pig... then turn around and continue walking towards me, no hurry like. Pick up your shotgun slowly as you return, but *don't* point it at them whatever you do. We'll both then wave goodbye to 'em and clear out.'

'Right you are,' Harry whispered, albeit not feeling as confident as he sounded.

Back at their camp, Harry said, 'That was all a bit sad really. I didn't intend to upset anyone yah know, Patrick, and I'll be buggered if I saw them in the long grass, did you?'

'No, not until they stood up, right next to you!'

'Just as well you arrived when you did, mate. To reload, I don't reckon I'd have had time to use my pocketknife and reload before they nailed me good and proper!'

* * *

RATHER THAN RETURN the same way to Albury, Patrick suggested they head south and cross the Murray River back into Victoria at the first opportunity.

As evening approached and the red gums again began to dominate their surroundings, Patrick's horse, which was leading, stopped suddenly and whinnied a warning.

Immediately alert, Harry eased himself up from his saddle, leather squeaking as he did so and sniffed the air. 'I can smell smoke, can you?'

'Yes, just. Do you want to investigate or have you had enough excitement for today?'

'Nah, I'm good. Let's check it out, it's probably a farmhouse. Perhaps we can cadge a cuppa or something to eat maybe?'

It wasn't long before they realised that the origin of the smoke was not coming from a farmhouse, but from a clearing where two young men sat around a small fire, obviously waiting for their billy to boil.

Not to alarm the men, Harry and Patrick dismounted and in full view casually led their three horses into the clearing. The reception they received was definitely *not* what they expected.

Both men jumped to their feet and threw their hands above their heads in an obvious surrender; one farting loudly in the process, the other mumbling... '*Oh shit!*, we're goners now for sure!'

'Easy now lads,' said Harry, 'we're not the traps so put your hands down and relax for Christ's sake.'

Patrick quickly added, hoping to put them at ease. 'Have you got the makings for four cups of tea? If not, we have and I can tell you, we're parched. My name's Patrick and this is Harry. By what names do you go by, lads?'

Harry was now seated, which encouraged them all to sit. However, it was obvious both fellows had been crying; old tear stains ran down their dusty cheeks. And occasionally, both swept snot from their top lip.

While Harry fussed around preparing tea and retrieved some biscuits from their packhorse's saddle bags, Patrick sat quietly watching them. Both seemed healthy, strong and athletic. Yet both were visibly traumatised.

'Come on lads, life can't be that bad. How old are you anyway?'

'Alright, if yah must know, I'm Dan and he's Steve. I'm goin' on twenty and he's twenty-three... and well, we're both in shitter's ditch and we thought you'se were the traps.'

'Well we're not,' said Harry as he handed mugs of sweetened black tea to each lad.

As they all sat quietly sipping their tea and eagerly dunked their biscuits, Patrick continued to observe the young men. Steve was not as tall as Dan and slightly less well built. His hair was brown, of medium length which bore the semblance of being centrally parted.

Both wore clothes that had obviously seen much better days.

Steve maintained a sort of aloofness; his otherwise youthful and tanned face held an unsettling, vindictive expression. *He's troubled, this one*, Patrick thought.

Dan on the other hand had a sallow face, a shock of jet-black hair, but had little facial hair, which belied his age. Though he seemed to be the one making decisions, he now appeared to have a quiet, yet morose temperament.

'So lads, what on earth has put the wind up yah?' Harry asked quietly.

'Look, we've been on the run from time to time, too,' Patrick added, 'but we are *not* the police or their deputies, so you are not under threat from us.' This language, combining a tone of compassion and subtle persuasion, soon unlocked Steve's tongue.

'Yeah, well, we somehow escaped from a gunfight; and now the entire bloody Victorian police force are looking for us we think. First, they killed our best friend, Joe, and shot and seriously wounded Dan's brother, Ned... then arrested him. And as far as we know they railed Ned off to jail in Melbourne... so that'll be the last we'll ever see of him alive!'

'And you were *both* involved in that shootout?' Harry probed.

'Yeah. We had a go at shootin' as many coppers as we could, but the body armour we built that was supposed to protect us turned out to be bloody useless.

'There were far too many coppers around to fight on; there was hundreds of the bastards, I reckon. So, we took a punt and bolted.

'Luckily, some sympathisers of Ned that we knew well, shoved us onto some horses—those over there—and so we scarpered. With all the bullets flyin' everywhere, I'll be forever buggered if I know how we got away, but we did.

'And here we are now, two weeks on, scared shitless that the traps will shoot us on sight or that we'll starve to death right here.

'We've got nothing to eat and have no hope of getting any food unless we steal it... but from where, we're totally lost.'

'You really are in shitter's ditch, eh lads,' Harry chuckled, 'but I reckon we know who you are and perhaps we can help. Just last week Patrick and me read about a siege down south at a place called Glenrowan, I believe.

'Apparently the cops nailed your brother really good; isn't that right, Dan? He was certainly an interesting and pretty determined chap if I believe everything I read.'

'Yes, he was... and you're right, I'm Dan Kelly, his brother. What else do you want to know?'

'According to the newspaper, it reckons you two were supposed to have been burnt to a crisp in that pub,' said Patrick, 'but here both you are, alive and no doubt bitter. Want to tell us how you got here?'

'Later, if you don't mind,' said Steve. 'And my name's Steve Hart, as you've probably guessed. But we desperately need to eat something or we'll be dead come dawn tomorrow. Can you help us, or not?'

* * *

'IF HARRY or me ever hear that either one of you've dobbed us in for aiding and abetting you, as the law calls it, we'll find you and you'll die a far worse death than if we had never saved your poor backsides,' said Harry, as in turn, he shook hands with the now amply fed, no longer cashless and far less demoralised young men.

'Now get a move on and good luck,' Patrick added. 'But don't forget to contact our friend Robert Eames, in Gloucester, should you make it there. He'll put you right if you're square with him. Just mention to him that we sent you.

'And, if perchance you do fall back into shitter's ditch, remember to introduce yourselves to Gordon. He's another of our friends and he'll also put you right... but you'll need to visit the Trial Bay Jail to find him.'

* * *

'WELL THAT WAS MOST interesting and observant of you, Harry,' Patrick wisecracked.

'Now what say you, that we change our plans and get some well-earned peace and quiet. I do believe Echuca's not too far downstream from here, but first things first, we need to get onto the Victorian side of the river.'

'You'll get no grief from me on that score, Patrick.'

35

Their eventual arrival in Echuca was essentially ignored, and because the residents had no idea who they were, it therefore made Harry's and Patrick's visits to the assaying office and then securing a modest, centrally located rental cottage, of no significance to anyone. Or so they thought.

Not more than ten minutes' walk from their cottage, Harry and Patrick also located agistment for their horses. The paddock owner happily pocketed their one month's lease payment, then drew his customers into a friendly, albeit probing conversation. 'Nice bit of horse flesh you've got there boys. Me name's Roy, Roy Brownless; and you are?'

Being burdened by their saddles, halters, saddle bags and bridles made it impossible to shake hands, but Patrick said, 'I'm Patrick and me mate's, Harold. Shut the gate for us Roy, there's a good man. We're relying on you to keep a sharpish eye out for them, and should they disappear, it's going to be *your* neck in a noose if they do.'

'No need to concern yerselves, they're as safe as me own horses; that's them in the paddock next door to this. They're both thorough-breds and I'll be fielding both of 'em in Saturday's races, here in

Echuca. Actually this 'ere is a bloody good track and well suited to my two.

'Yours is Walers, I'd say. Not much to look at, but they sure seem to be in good nick. How'd yah get 'em lookin' so fit?'

'Just hard work,' Harry replied. 'They've carted us halfway across this country. Can't stay and chat, mate. This gear is bloody heavy and we need to get it home before night sets in. We'll talk again later, eh?'

While the men stored the horses' tackle, Patrick said casually, 'do you know what Harry? I do believe our friend, Roy, just might be setting us up for a fall, *or perhaps* some fun...'

'He seems alright to me, but I'll always concede to your nous on such matters.' After a thoughtful pause, Harry continued. 'You don't suppose Roy wants us to have a go at winning a race or two with *our somewhat inferior Walers* on the weekend?'

'He's a local and probably already knows how good the opposition are, and we don't. But if he underestimates ours, particularly if we enter them in the longest event, some folks just might get an unwelcome surprise.

'C'mon Harry, it's tempting you must agree, and it should be a bit of fun so long as we don't waste our hard-earned on stupid bets. I've been told police usually attend all country race meetings, so we'll need to avoid them just in case they get nosey. I also read somewhere that that Kelly Gang often frequented country race meetings, yet somehow always managed to avoid the police. But that was then; things are likely to be different now.

'So Harry, my good man, if you're in, best we get organised and find out how we enter our horses and what sort of prize money's being offered. Regardless, we'll need a capable jockey; we're both well over a sensible racing weight.'

'Yeah, I'm in. But surely, we're at a disadvantage with our saddles; they're nothing like proper racing saddles.'

* * *

ON THE ONE hand Harry and Patrick were a little disappointed that all three of their horses could not be accepted to run in the one and a half mile Echuca Cup, the last race of the meeting. There was only one place remaining in that event resulting from a scratching, necessary because of a serious unloading injury to one of the entrants. On the other hand, they were content that their two other horses were accepted for another feature race, albeit one of only one mile.

Their acceptance fees having been paid, they set off to find a jockey, but were unexpectedly delayed by their new acquaintance, Roy, who called them over to inspect the Echuca Cup trophy.

'Not bad, eh,' he said, gloating as if it was already his. 'The good oil, my friends, is that she'll be on my mantelpiece by sundown on Saturday. And mind you, the five hundred quid that comes with the trophy will be most welcome. So don't be too disappointed. You can still make yerselves a few quid on mine, with the on-course bookies, even though the odds'll be shortish, like.'

Harry and Patrick were initially disheartened because they could not find a suitable jockey, so much so they were about to give up. However, most unexpectedly, an aboriginal girl, about sixteen years old, walked confidently towards them carrying a jockey's racing saddle and a matching bridle.

'G'day fellas, I've heard you'd been lookin' for a jockey; you still interested?'

'Absolutely,' replied Patrick, 'so what's your name and tell us a bit about yourself. Oh, and this gentleman is my mate, Harry.'

'Not, Harold?'

'No, I'm Harry. You've been talking with Roy, yeah?'

'Yeah, he's not a nice fella, that. I worked for him once, last year, but he refused to pay me my cut of the prize money I won him... not for months, anyway. An' he kept callin' me "a black bitch"!

'So, he can bloody well go jump in a lake. My name's Rosey; and you're...?'

'Patrick,' Patrick, said as he warmly shook Rosey's hand. Right, that's settled. Just tell us what you want and that you'll do your absolute best and we have a deal. We can only offer you two rides, Rosey. Is that alright with you? By the way, what do you weigh?'

'Ahh now, that's for you to guess and for our opposition to worry about. And two rides is fine, thanks.'

Harry then stepped forward to shake Rosey's hand and while doing so, playfully gabbed her right bicep. 'Bloody Hell, with muscles like this you could tame wild bulls, I reckon.'

'I've ridden a few in my time,' replied Rosey, smiling, 'but c'mon, we're wasting time standing here. I need to meet your horses and you've got a lot to tell me about 'em.'

* * *

As FORECAST, Cup Day dawned warm with a northerly breeze gently rolling over the racetrack and its environs. A good crowd was expected and likely to grow as the afternoon unfolded.

When the racecourse gates were thrown open, many voices soon competed to be heard, punctuated by occasional outbursts of laughter and the ever-courageous bookmakers shouting their early "best odds" from beneath their improvised, canvas covered betting ring.

The on-course mood was already festive, made even more so by a local band determined to not only showcase their solo instrument playing skills, but to faultlessly play their collective, well-rehearsed medley of catchy tunes.

Most of the horses were tethered in the shade cast by several tall eucalypts. Grooms patiently brushed, washed, dried and currycombed, water carriers scurried about, farriers checked hooves and owners scrutinized everything with an equal measure of self-importance, well-practiced oversight and an eagerness to see their beautifully turned-out steeds perform.

A crowd had soon gathered around Roy's two thoroughbreds for they were indeed magnificent looking and beautifully presented animals.

Most punters however, wandered straight by Harry's and Patrick's horses. Roy also strolled by, smiled condescendingly, harrumphed and said, 'don't waste your dough, boys. Yah surely don't really think yours can win, do yah?' He then shrugged his shoulders and walked away, slowly shaking his head.

However, Harry and Patrick smiled benevolently to each other, mimicking Roy's shoulder shrug and head nodding.

Rosey, not to be put off, raised both her hands, each directing a very rigid index finger salute toward Roy's retreating back. 'We'll see; yah no good, cocky bastard,' Rosey muttered.

36

One race, two entrants and only one jockey? This was the conundrum still facing Harry and Patrick... and only two hours before race time. Scratch one of their own horses? Hope that another owner might need to scratch theirs in the nick of time, thereby allowing Harry and Patrick to have first call on that disadvantaged jockey?

Patrick had gone quiet, weighing up their options when an idea struck him. Out of earshot from Rosey, he nudged Harry and said discreetly, 'I think I've got it! Not strictly legal of course, but money talks, eh?'

'Go on, this had better be good,' Harry replied, obviously interested but alert to potentially hidden consequences.

'Well, we could bribe one of the owners. Hang on, hang on, let me finish. If we offered an inducement to the owner of a horse that has no chance of winning, I reckon he'd roll over, particularly if we offered him a few more quid than he would get *if he actually did win the race*. We're carrying plenty of coin and can pay him off to leave the track immediately and to say nothing to anyone, other than announcing his scratching to the stewards.'

'Yeah, and you'd want me to convince him in no uncertain fashion to keep his trap shut, real tight like?'

'Well, yes of course, but you'd need to exercise your usual discretion.

'We'd also pay the owner for any late withdrawal fees and of course the original fee his jockey was promised... and we'd then pay that jockey an even bigger fee to switch rides.

'The biggest problem we've got as I see it, is that we'd have to execute my plan *before* the bookmakers set their boards. So, what say you, Harry, we revert to our unsociable bushrangin' ways for a bit of fun, or...?'

'Alright, alright, let's do it, but what do we tell Rosey?'

'We tell her all, because we need to see how she'll react. C'mon, we're wasting time.'

* * *

ROSEY GIGGLED at Patrick's audacious plan, adding, 'Go for it, I've seen worse. Besides, it's got nothin' to do with me. Good luck, but you know I'll be trying to beat your other nag, eh?'

Patrick's hastily conceived plan caused barely a ripple as the bookmakers and punters accepted the field change, and their second jockey, though bemused, was most thankful he'd not forfeit anything and that he'd arrive home with a few quid in his pocket for a change.

* * *

WITH PRIZE MONEY set at two hundred pounds and the expectation of a tight race, not only were the punters excited, but an intense sense of rivalry had gripped some of the jockeys. In the mounting yard, disrespectful challenges were being hotly exchanged.

At the drop of the starting flag, cheers of encouragement erupted from the crowd and soon after the initial release melee, Roy's jockey pushed his magnificent mount into a commanding early lead.

The track, leading from the starting line to the first right hand bend, soon became hidden by trees and undergrowth which continued that way for at least a third of the entire circuit. The trailing horses leaving that bend belonged to Patrick and Harry... and were at least ten lengths last.

When the field emerged from the scrub, a significant change had occurred. Although Roy's horse was still leading, its lead had reduced to just two lengths and appeared to be tiring. And just five lengths back was Rosey, holding Patrick's horse to a steady pace.

At the homeward bend, Patrick's and Harry's Walers had moved to within a length of Roy's flagging thoroughbred and it was becoming obvious that the punters were to witness a spectacular finish.

At last, Rosy firmly booted Patrick's horse. It responded immediately and in a surge, drew level and was thus well placed to capture the lead.

Just then, something most unexpectedly happened! Rosey abruptly slumped to her left and only by the grace of the racing gods stayed in her saddle.

Roy's horse won, but almost fell over the winning line from exhaustion. Harry's horse charged past to finish second and somehow Rosey got Patrick's horse over the line to finish third.

Some punters were ecstatic, others booed loudly, others shouted obscenities and screamed...*"protest!"*.

Patrick and Harry were the first owners into the winner's ring. Harry quickly took charge of his horse, while congratulating his jockey, but strangely, the jockey simply nodded and dismounted, apparently underwhelmed by the proceedings and clearly annoyed.

Rosey didn't wait for Patrick to help her dismount, she slipped to the ground and stormed off holding her face, not bothering to collect her saddle. 'Rosey! Stop!' Patrick yelled as he ran after her, then firmly grabbed her arm.

'Good God, Rosey,' Patrick pleaded gently, as she swung around to face him. 'Are you alright, girl? What the hell happened to your face? Talk to me. What the hell happened?'

Tears weren't far from Rosey's eyes as she removed her hand from her face to reveal a bleeding welt that extended from her forehead to her chin.

Patrick immediately embraced Rosey, not caring what any onlookers might think as he said quietly, 'you have my word, my dear girl, that the bastard who did this to you is about to wish he'd never been born.'

As they stepped apart, Harry, who had run over to see what was transpiring, looked aghast at Rosey's bleeding face. Initially he said nothing, he just fumed and gritted his teeth, but then asked, 'Was it Roy's jockey that kicked your foot out of your stirrup and slashed your face with his whip?'

Rosy nodded. Harry mimicked her nod knowingly, then stormed off.

Comforting Rosey with his arm firmly around her waist, Patrick led her to the on-course first-aid tent and demanded immediate attention.

Half an hour later, just as the doctor was putting the finishing touches to Rosey's wound, an attendant rushed into the tent. 'Doc, doc. Come quick! There's been a stoush and two fellas is in a real bad way. One might even be dead!'

The doctor immediately grabbed his medical bag and said, 'alright, alright, stay calm. You'll be fine young lady, just keep that wound clean. Now, lead on sir and be quick about it.

Following the doctor, Patrick grabbed Rosey's hand and ran to the winner's ring where a somewhat sombre crowd had gathered. They pushed their way through the crowd and were met by an interesting scene.

There sat Harry, happily chatting to three suited gentlemen, obviously plain clothes police, all chuckling while taking notes.

However, to one side and contrary to the conviviality of those four men, was a very different spectacle: there lay Roy and his dodgy jockey, both barely conscious, bruised and bleeding profusely.

The doctor soon proclaimed that they would both live, but that they needed urgent hospital treatment. After that announcement, nobody in the surrounding spectator crowd seemed interested in helping; to most, the fun was over, so they just meandered away, now only interested in placing their next bets.

* * *

'WHAT ON EARTH did you hit them with, Harry? A four by two?'

'Nah, just these,' Harry replied, holding up his fists and both of his booted feet.

'Did you know that Roy wore dentures? Not much use to him now. And I don't suppose you could've noticed that that little shit has a bad limp? I think his leg's broken, poor bugger, eh?

'Those coppers were good blokes; got a sense of humour, and they'll see to it that charges are laid on those two arseholes.'

'And you, Harry, what did the coppers promise you?'

'"Timely retribution." They used that word a few times. I think it means "Squaring the ledger", or something like that. Roy's going to forfeit any winnings and his jockey will not see this racetrack again. Anyway, those coppers reckoned I did *them* a favour, givin' those two what they've both been deservin' for years.

'All three cops saw what happened and agreed with me that Rosey could have been killed. They want to charge 'em both with attempted murder. Apparently, they've already interviewed several witnesses so I won't be needed to attend court for the trial. Yeah, I'm bloody lucky, but I reckon it's time to say goodbye to Echuca; the sooner the better, eh?'

'Not before we have a go at winning that Cup,' said a very determined Rosey.

Out of Rosey's hearing range as the men set about preparing their packhorse for its run in the Echuca Cup, Patrick said, 'I say, Harry, that girl is sure made of tough stuff. She'll always be a champion in my eyes, regardless of who wins the damn cup.'

'Agreed. Pity Roy's not going to see the race,' said Harry sarcastically, 'his horse does look the goods. You going to have a bet, Patrick?'

'Yep. And most of anything I might win, I'm giving to Rosey.'

* * *

THE RACE WAS A CRACKER. Rosey rode their Waler at an almost sedate clip, oblivious to the crowd who were urging on the favourite. Again, her mount was the last to leave sight as the field disappeared behind the wall of scrub along the back straight.

Once back in sight, the crowd resumed their urging of the favourite with significantly more gusto, knowing that Roy's thorough-bred had excellent staying credentials.

In fact, it did everything right—except win—even though it led by nearly eight lengths as the field passed the one-mile marker. Within sight of the winning post and as if by magic, the leading horses tired badly, spread and fell back, leaving Rosey a clear run to the winning post.

Although Roy's "last minute *replacement* jockey" was frantically flogging the favourite, Rosey's horse charged through an enticing gap and in just a few strides was running neck to neck, but with more purpose than the previously unchallenged favourite.

With only a handful of strides remaining, Rosey squeezed the Waler urgently with her calf muscles. It responded, yet again, surging ahead to win by a long head.

Harry and Patrick stared at each other in disbelief. 'Bloody hell, did you see that?' Harry screamed, then jumped about while maniacally waving his arms above his head. But when he turned to congratulate his friend, Patrick was nowhere to be seen.

The penny quickly dropped. Harry raced to be with Patrick when Rosey led the field back to the winner's circle.

As Rosey dismounted and although still puffing heavily from her exertions, she was beside herself, beaming a huge joyful smile and yelled, 'I told you we could do it. I knew it! All along I knew your horse could win; that extra half mile did the trick. All three of your Walers are amazing; I love them so much!'

'Never doubted you'd not win,' replied Patrick. 'The trophy's yours you little champ, a keepsake from us and we'll see to it that it's your name on that trophy, not ours.'

'And the prize money's all yours,' Harry chimed in. 'besides, we both made more than enough from our bets, so don't worry about us.'

'And don't go wasting it,' Patrick added. "Look after it and you'll be able to visit Europe or America whenever it suits you. And then Rosey... you can show the world just how good a rider you really are.'

37

H aving hosed, watered and curry-combed their horses and farewelled Rosey, Patrick and Harry nonchalantly walked them back to the agistment paddock. 'No padlocks,' Harry commented somewhat unnecessarily as he led the horses through the gate and back into the paddock.

'Unnecessary now, I'd say,' replied Patrick. 'I don't think Roy will be up to doing anything devious, given what you did to him today. In fact, I don't think he'll know what day it is for some time. Which, my friend, gives us ample time to pack and to keep our animals well fed until we move on.'

'Right, so let's get down to that tavern beside the river and celebrate,' said Harry. 'I don't know exactly how much I've won from my bets, but it must be nudgin' four hundred quid. And you Patrick?'

'I don't believe I won quite that much; maybe two fifty. Therefore it'll be your shout when we get to the tavern. However, my friend, I'll buy you your dinner, no matter what you fancy... just because you're an amazing young fellow even when you're *not* keeping your nose clean.'

'What a day. You know what, Patrick? I'll never expect to win anything as grand as today's takings. How'd we actually pull that off anyway?'

'With your best friend's cunning, Harry my good man. And perhaps with just a sprinkle of mischief, your special form of payback and a lovely aboriginal girl's determination and courage.'

'Nicely put old chap, but come on, I'm parched... and I could eat a horse and chase the rider.'

'How fitting; a saying for every occasion. How'd you come by so many?'

'You mostly, but those bullockies back at Copeland run a close second.'

Still laughing, they entered the riverside tavern, commandeered a table with a view of the river and the jetty, ordered their dinner then sagged into their chairs to down their first cool beer for the evening.

An hour later, Harry's earlier musings of his unbeatably good luck and prosperity were about to be proven wrong... and subsequently further change his life forever.

As for Patrick... well?

* * *

As NIGHT gently cast its cloak over the glowing remnants of a magnificent sunset, Harry stood on the tavern's verandah, admiring the river and inhaling the fragrances of the riverside eucalypts; the fading daylight softening this momentous day.

He would have preferred to savour some quiet time in his own company to reflect further upon the day's events. And he would have done so but for the flocks of boisterous cockatoos departing to their roosts... and for the distant sound of a paddle steamer making its approach to Albury's famous river port.

Harry watched, sipping the last of his beer. He admired how the skipper with great skill manoeuvered the paddle steamer alongside the jetty, where, then with the help of two jetty hands quickly had the vessel safely secured.

Several passengers were lining the deck's handrails, all clearly impatient to get on land. Within minutes it seemed that the last of them had disembarked, however, some lingered on the jetty waiting for their crates of belongings to be carried ashore.

Thinking there would be no more action, Harry was about to return inside to the tavern bar for just one last beer, when another movement caught his eye.

Two passengers, struggling to carry their bags, almost fell onto the paddle steamer's deck. Both were women, and very fetching... and despite the low light cast by the boat's fuel lamps and the passing of many long years since they parted company in Fremantle, he immediately recognised them.

Harry jumped down the steps of the tavern and raced across the jetty. 'Good God almighty, it *is* you... *Jane*? Right? And your mum, isn't it?'

'Yes, it's me alright. I'm Maddy, remember?'

Without another word being spoken, Jane dropped her bags and not taking her eyes from Harry, walked demurely up to him and stopped barely an inch from his chest.

In one almost imperceptible movement, she then rested her body upon Harry's chest while gently placing the palms of her hands on his cheeks, her eyes probing his, just as she had done when they first met.

But on this occasion Harry was very aware of, and could now feel the soft, unmistakable swelling of Jane's breasts. 'Harry, my darling handsome man,' Jane whispered, 'I've thought about you every damn day. I just knew we'd have to meet again. At last! Please promise me you'll never leave me again.'

With equal finesse, Jane then drew Harry's face down to be level with hers and then, as if panicked, planted a most sensual kiss firmly upon his lips.

This time, Harry responded with equal urgency and without inhibition. So enthralled was he that he wasn't initially aware of the tingling in his gentleman's region. 'You know I'll never leave you, you gorgeous girl; I've only just found you again,' was the best that Harry could mutter while luxuriating in the promise of even closer intimacy.

'If you don't mind, you two,' said Maddy in a knowing but impatient tone, 'I really would like to get our baggage off this vessel. And would you please unhand my daughter, Harry, so that we can get along to our lodgings.'

Both almost breathless, they broke their embrace, yet continued staring into each other's eyes while shamelessly blocking the gangway.

'Bloody Hell, Harry,' said Patrick who had been watching from the tavern as this scene unfolded, 'you're the sneakiest chap I've *ever* known. I leave you alone for just five minutes and you've somehow pirated these beautiful women into your clutches. For heaven's sake, move so I can get these ladies' belongings onto the jetty.'

Eventually Patrick placed the last case onto the jetty. 'Ah, that's the one I've been looking for. Now ladies, let me introduce myself, then we should make tracks to wherever you need to go. I'm Patri...'

'Don't bother Patrick, we know who you are', Maddy interrupted, 'But do you know who I am, pray tell?'

'Yes, indeed I do. You're Maddison and you've not changed one little bit, my fair lady. And if I'm not mistaken this can only be Jane, your equally beautiful daughter.' Had it not been quite so dark, you could not have missed the unmistakable spark of attraction between Maddy and Patrick.

A little later, while Harry and Patrick were sizing up the job of carrying the ladies' baggage, and just out of earshot from them, Harry whispered, 'how'd yah get on board by the way?'

'Well, you were so obviously overjoyed to be rekindling an old flame. You also seemed somewhat inconvenienced and had no intention of unhanding Jane, or moving, so I just jumped from the jetty onto the boat's deck... all quick smart and Cupid like.'

38

It was only a short walk of three hundred yards or so to Maddy's and Jane's cottage. Harry and Jane were leading, while Maddy and Patrick lagged: all shared as equally as possible the women's luggage that they had accumulated since arriving in Australia.

'How long have you lived here?' Harry asked excitedly as he held the front gate open for the others to pass through into the front yard. 'We arrived here just a week ago and we're no more than a couple of hundred yards from here. How about that!"

'We've been here going on three years,' Maddy replied, 'but first let's get inside and unpack and put the kettle on, then all can be revealed. I'm predicting that should be a bit fun.

'Jane, you know where everything is, would you please light the lamps and get the stove going? I hope you haven't lost the front door key.'

'*No* mum. Well come on, get cracking or it'll be dawn before we get settled! Would you check our mailbox please, Patrick? And Harry, my darling, follow me please. You can help me collect any eggs. I'll get some kindling and if you would please, you can carry in some heavier bits of wood.'

'Oh heavens, I do hope Mr Forbes has been collecting our eggs while we've been away *and* remembered to leave us a few,' Maddy added, 'otherwise it'll be tea and biscuits only for supper I'm afraid.'

* * *

As the evening unfolded it became obvious the easy, general conversation, laughter and occasional gravity was more than just friendship, far more.

Loneliness may have played its part, but the forward-looking attitude of the women perfectly complimented the men's understated achievements and mutual desire to continue their travels.

In the hours that ensued, Patrick and Harry listened as Maddison and Jane took it in turn to outline their most recent history since parting company in Fremantle.

Yet, at the first opportunity when Patrick and Harry found themselves alone for a few minutes, Patrick said quietly, 'Harry my dear man, whatever you say, I'd prefer that you said *absolutely nothing* about our success at Copeland; just for the time being anyway. The right time for that will present itself soon enough. Regardless, at this moment my sense of trust is not being taxed, but now is not the time to be volunteering that we are both free, yet very grateful thieves.

'Oh, one other thing, Harry. Did you get a chance to browse through yesterday's local paper when we were at the tavern?'

'No, why?'

'Well I did and it seems we might be on thin ice. Apparently, Mike Dudley, that New South Wales detective chap, was quoted as saying he's received positive sightings of his two suspects and now knows their whereabouts. Reckons he'll be arriving in Echuca in a few weeks' time, where he anticipates making an arrest or two. That sounds like us, my friend.'

'That may well be, Patrick, but I'm telling you right now, he'll have his work cut out if he expects to deny me of *my* freedom.'

* * *

THAT NIGHT, Patrick and Harry learnt that Maddy, within a week of arriving in the township of Adelaide, purchased her own cottage. Both mother and daughter obviously loved Adelaide. Maddy soon found that her skills in the banking world were still held in high esteem and quickly found work, while Jane held no reservations about attending school.

Three years later, Maddy heard on the grapevine that a potentially lucrative teaching job was up for grabs in Mildura; including free accommodation.

She applied for the job and a month later mother and daughter were established in a traditional rural school setting catering not only for white children, but for any unregistered local indigenous children who just walked in. Jane enjoyed helping her mother and became firm friends with everyone.

Unfortunately, Maddy found the long periods of hot weather very demanding and admitted failure to acclimatising.

By the grace of the "Education Gods" a regional school inspector took pity upon her and not wanting to lose such a capable educator, arranged for her to be transferred to Echuca where the climate was guaranteed to be more agreeable. And so, it was. Both mother and daughter fell in love with Echuca and three years later considered themselves locals.

However, Jane had become impatient to stamp her independence and though she continued to assist Maddy at the school, she was now looking to stretch her wings and pursue another career. Which accounted for Maddy and Jane coincidentally arriving at the Echuca port jetty as Patrick and Harry were celebrating their eventful day at the Echuca Cup; for both women had been downstream finalising a "Jillaroo" job for Jane at a homestead near to the twin riverside settlements of Barham and Koondrook.

When finally the last of their fire surrendered to the chill of the approaching dawn, Patrick and Harry rose reluctantly from their chairs and farewelled their hosts. No handshakes; a gentle kiss to each lady's cheek did more than just express thanks for their company.

As the two men made their way home in the false dawn, both were tired but elated.

'So Harry, perchance was *this* meeting better than winning the Echuca Cup?'

'No comparison. Even beats our windfall at Copeland. But hey, how much younger are you than Maddy? You both seem, well, fairly taken by each other.'

'Eight years. But if you believe I'm *fairly taken*, as you put it, you, and Jane *are*, my friend, *both totally out of control!*'

'Never saw that coming, did we, eh?' Harry replied philosophically.

* * *

OVER THE NEXT FEW WEEKS, many joyful reciprocal cottage visitations took place. It was during one of these meetings Harry and Patrick unburdened themselves of their theft of the Copeland goldmine's first gold shipment and the ensuing deaths of two bushrangers and two hapless government security policemen. Regardless, this revelation did nothing to dampen the women's unwavering love for their men.

Clearly, two poorly disguised love affairs were obviously at play, both of which soon morphed into natural, separate cohabitations.

39

'I say, Harry, I don't recall ever saying this to you, but, well, I need your undivided attention for a few minutes.'

'In that tone of voice, I know as sure as duck's lay eggs you're about to unburden something serious, so go on Patrick, out with it.'

'Alright, but first, let's sit here where only the river will hear us.

'As we are both aware, the feelings we have for our wonderful ladies mean a hell of a lot more than just casual friendships. So much so in my case that I've asked Maddy to marry me... and she accepted. How about that, eh?'

'What in God's name took you so long? I'm not surprised though. Mind you, you've somehow not only convinced Maddy that you are no longer a rogue, or anymore a thief, or an unpunished bushranger, but rather, that you're the most amazing, reliable and trustworthy friend anyone could ever wish for. But obviously you did, so well done and my sincerest congratulations my friend,' said Harry as he offered his hand.

'A lovely speech, Harry, and thank you; at least I've taught you something. But hang on a minute! What did you *really* mean by "*me* taking so long"?'

'*Well, I proposed to Jane a week ago!* And yes, she accepted too: how about that! I've been bursting for the right time to tell yah.'

'I don't believe I've ever felt so proud of you, Harry, you're going to make a grand husband and an even better father of countless children. And thank you for covering my back on so many occasions.'

After a pause filled with elation and reflection, Patrick said quietly, 'Regrettably, things are about to change, Harry, in many ways, ways in which neither of us ever believed possible.

'I don't mean anything sinister by that remark, just that we owe our "beautiful wives to be", not only our never-ending love and our respect and gratitude, but more importantly, we must provide for their ongoing safety; that's paramount, eh?'

'But Harry, you also need to know that we are leaving Echuca and will probably never return. Maddy's on the verge of selling her cottage and we hope to be on our way in about seven days.

'Maddy admits she still loves Adelaide and misses the many friends she left behind. And as good luck dictates, her old boss is ecstatic at the prospect of having her back at his bank and her brother and his family are now residents there. I also understand that Adelaide is made up entirely of free settlers.'

'Good God, you two haven't missed a beat, have you?' replied Harry, somewhat shocked by the pace of developments. 'Mate, you'll always land on your feet, but what the hell will you do with yourself? You'll surely get bored within five minutes.'

'Not necessarily. You see, apparently, Maddy's brother is a keen sailor and would love to start his own boat building business, so I might be able to offer my services; after all, I did spend nearly six years in the Marines and I'm bound to tumble upon mischief somewhere. But rest easy, I'll never jeopardise, Maddy.'

'And Jane, has she been told of your plans yet?'

'That's probably happening as we speak,' Patrick replied with just a hint of conspiracy. 'Maddy is taking Jane shopping on the pretence that she wants her opinion on a selection of new shrubs for the front garden of their cottage. But in fact, by now, they will have found their way to that posh tea shop near the tavern, where *all* will be revealed.

'Just one more thing, Harry; that bloody detective. We need to get moving, and fast, if my gut feeling is correct. We still hold an ace up our sleeves by going our own separate ways; he can't be in two places at once.

'It's likely he'll continue to pursue one of us, but he'll be chasing two respectable married couples down two proverbial rabbit burrows. And if we get a move on, you'll be in Victoria and I'll be in South Australia where he has no jurisdiction. Regardless, we'll both have to keep our guard up against unexpected surprises... that's the inevitability of our lot from now on, eh?'

* * *

WHAT THE NEWSPAPERS couldn't tell their readers was that Inspector Dudley never made it to Echuca. His intuition, persistence and subsequent deductions regarding Harry's and Patrick's whereabouts had been spot on. Just what Teddy Green wanted: they were closing in on their elusive quarry... and *his* gold. Yes *his* gold; the object of his current existence... the rightful reward for his previous meticulous planning, his daring in confronting and killing the troopers who guarded the gold shipment and for suffering the ignominious loss of his freedom.

At that time, Teddy's questionable good luck took another most unexpected turn. Not only had he gleaned sufficient information from Mike to have a firm trace on Harry's and Patrick's most likely location, but *he* no longer had to kill Mike to ensure that when the gold was recovered, it would *all* be his!

Uncannily, it transpired one evening, after Mike finished bathing in the Murray River and was in the process of clambering up the river's slippery bank, that he was struck twice in quick succession by a deadly tiger snake.

Teddy witnessed the incident but refused to offer any assistance as the snake's powerful venom took control of Mike's senses and movements.

'Serves you right, copper,' Teddy muttered as he booted Mike back into the river. 'Yah just too lenient for your own good.'

Without either compassion or regret, Teddy watched, smiling, as Inspector Mike Dudley's body was dragged to mid-river. 'Good riddance, yah dopey bastard,' he added as Mike's body gradually sank, to be swept away to God only knew where.

Pleased with that outcome, Teddy continued muttering to himself as he walked away from the river. 'And I've now got your money, your nag, your rifle and your handgun, so who's the clever dick now?'

40

———

Harry volunteered to help Patrick and Maddy pack, crate and load their household goods and furniture, but Patrick had a surprise in store. 'No need mate, unless something has either sentimental value or is of unreplaceable or practical value to Maddy, then it stays here. Thanks for offering anyway. Besides, I can easily afford to buy our own house in Adelaide and pay for whatever Maddy needs—and wants—to fill it with furniture and mod cons and barely put a dint it my funds.

'On the other hand, I think you're the one going to need help getting rid of Jane's belongings. They can't be left in our rented cottage before Maddy's place sells. Someone is bound to get suspicious and perhaps dob us in when they're found. No, you should either burn everything or bury it somewhere well out of sight. I'll leave that up to you two, but whatever you decide, please do it quickly and soon!'

'Which reminds me,' Harry replied, 'will you be taking your horse with you?'

'No, they're all yours now, or Jane's. The packhorse, our secret and magnificent cup winner, is yours to boot. They've been wonderful company, eh? I'll miss them; they're all so unbelievably even-

174

tempered and gallant; never shirked anything we asked of them, eh? But, my friend, I know you'll treat them well.'

'Thanks Patrick, but don't worry, you don't need my word that I'll take good care of 'em. And yes, they're a remarkable breed alright.'

'Oh, by the way, Harry, I noticed that our slimy friend, Roy, has moved his thoroughbreds and left our horses with not much of a pick. So how about we start looking for new agistment for the next few days?'

Unexpectedly for Harry, those few words triggered within his soul a sense of impending, brutal loss.

* * *

'So, my darling, what now?' Jane whispered to Harry as tears ran down his handsome face; his hands by his sides, it now being futile to continue waving because the paddle steamer was almost around the first downstream bend and about to disappear into the river's thick early morning mist.

Harry's tears were contagious and Jane could not hide hers any longer, nor could she disguise or control either her whimpering or grief. Somehow, she mumbled, 'do you think we'll ever see them again, Harry?'

'I hope to God we do, but right now my gut feeling tells me that that's it.'

Determined to shake off their sadness, Jane wrapped an arm around Harry's waist and steered him back to their cottage where she put on the kettle to make a cuppa.

As if it had only just occurred to her, she spun around and said excitedly, 'Harry, Patrick's right. We must make our own plans to travel, and soon. I reckon anywhere south would be great; just you and me and our horses. What do you think?'

'You'd be happy doing that? Really? It could get rough and what about when it's raining and freezing and we can't make a hot brew because we've run out of matches? And Jane, we won't be married! Mind you, we'd probably be much safer.'

'Married or not, that's *exactly* what I want to do. And I fear nothing, for I'll have you. Now, if you please, let's get back to bed.

'But before we do, I've got something important to tell you, my love. You see, mum pleaded with me to keep a little secret until after she and Patrick had departed. Well I did, but now I can tell you: mum thinks she's pregnant! Given her age, isn't that the most marvellous thing to happen right now?'

Silence reigned. Then, as that incredible information settled upon Harry, he finally spoke. 'Good God Almighty, Jane, they haven't wasted any time, eh? You're right, it's fantastic news and I'm so proud of Patrick, and Maddy, of course. I'd love to be a fly on the wall when Maddy breaks the news. I know that she's in the right hands, but Patrick might need to reassess his understanding of boredom.'

After much laughter and expansive lovemaking, Harry gently asked, 'Jane, what was your father like and what became of him?'

'He died when I was about three years old. His name was Joseph Stanley, but preferred to be called, Stan. He was a beaut dad, always seemed happy as I recall and he taught me how to ride and how to look after horses because he too loved them so much.

'But one day he never came home at the usual time, instead, the coppers did, carrying seriously bad news. Apparently, da was crushed when unloading beer kegs at the local pub. Died instantly, according to ma. It must've been dreadful for her; ma just cried and cried. But do you know what, Harry?'

'Yes, I think I do, Harry interrupted, 'you're going to tell me *that time cures all.'*

'Well, yes, I'd normally agree. But what makes it so frustrating is that ma suffered his loss so badly and for so long, because there was not the slightest sense of justice involved in da's unexpected death.'

'So why do you maintain that?'

'Because da never drank an alcoholic drink in his life!'

'Ehhhmm,' Harry mused, 'that's sad alright. I think I'd like to have met him. But, my dearest, right now, we honestly don't have time to reminisce... we must finish packing and be on our way tomorrow afternoon at the latest.'

Despite recurring bouts of nausea during the following day, she had gallantly mounted her horse in unison with Harry and rode side-by-side with her man, away from Echuca, into a glorious setting sun.

* * *

Six months later *Patrick Robert Taylor* arrived, his hearty good health a blessing, making life on the road tolerable for both of his devoted parents. Only occasionally did Jane express how inadequate she felt when confronted with the vagaries and essential needs of their infant son, but she never complained. Harry agreed how nice it would have been if Maddy was travelling with them, but she had enough on her hands and besides she was many hundreds of miles away.

41

'Harry?'

'Yes, Jane? What's on your mind?'

'Well we're not that far from Koondrook, where I was once expecting to start work... had you not turned up and put me in the family way.'

'That's your fault that by the way,' Harry replied with a mischievous smile, 'you shouldn't have taken so seriously what I only poked at you in fun.'

'Yea, yeah, well I'd like to revisit the nice folk who were going to employ me, the Woollers; you'd like them, I think. An unusual name, eh, given that they're sheep breeders? Besides, before Patrick and Maddy took off, I gave them the Woollers' postal address, just in case we ever passed through. Maybe, just maybe, there might be some mail for me to collect.'

'A long shot, but yeah, let's do it. Mind you, it's what, eight or nine months since Maddy and Patrick came this way.'

But as luck would have it, there was indeed a quite recent letter from Jane's mother awaiting collection, wherein Maddy proudly and foremostly announced that Jane now had a stepbrother, his name, *Stanley Harold Galbraith.*

Maddy also related that her term of pregnancy and the subsequent birth both went well; without complication and that she and young Stanley were in good health.

However, it seemed that Patrick, despite being overwhelmed, extremely proud and all thumbs, was manfully struggling to "*adjust*"... which she had underscored multiple times.

Harry read the first part of Maddy's letter, smiled broadly then handed it back to Jane. 'As we expected, great news, 'eh? When you write back, don't forget to give them my congratulations *and* to let them know *we three* are about to continue our journey, most likely to Melbourne.

'There's no point Maddy writing back to us though, not until after we get there, or wherever else we might decide to settle. Our letter will no doubt give 'em both something to think about, eh?'

'Yes, indeed it will, Harry, my love. If *we* write *our* return reply to them this minute, it can go on the paddle steamer's return journey to Adelaide first thing tomorrow morning.

'Oh, Harry, won't it be beaut to meet young Stanley and just incredible to be there when our boys eventually meet?'

'Yes, it most certainly will. But are you certain there was nothing in there about having unwelcome visitors?'

'No, absolutely nothing. Stop worrying, they'll be alright. Patrick would see to it if anything or anyone threatened them.'

A few weeks later, Harry and Jane, their son, Patrick Junior and their faithful three Walers headed into the remote northwest of Victoria.

* * *

THE FIRST PEOPLE Harry and Maddy encountered were two men, so intent upon repairing a section of fencing that they were unaware of visitors watching their efforts from a mere ten yards away.

'G'day there,' Harry called. 'Can I give you a hand, or would yah rather have a cuppa?'

The two men stopped working. One removed his hat then wiped

his forehead with the sleeve of his already sweat laden shirt while glaring at Harry. 'Nah, we'll be alright. Don't let us hold you up, it'll be getting dark pretty soon.'

'Whose fence yah fixing Bluey, yours or some poor bastards' whose cattle you've just nicked?'

'Let it go, darling,' Jane whispered urgently, 'these chaps are not our concern.'

'What sort of wise crack are you insinuating anyway, mister?' the man replied, not bothering to conceal his implied threat. 'Hang about; is that you Harry? It is! Well, I'll be buggered. How'd yah know it was me?

'By what's left of your hair, my friend,' Harry replied as he threw himself from his saddle and smiling broadly, walked up to Bluey. The two men were still shaking hands as Manfred walked over to join them.

'Bloody Hell, I thought we were done with you, Harry,' Manfred laughed while offering his hand in obvious friendship, 'but hey, where's Patrick?'

'No Patrick, he's in Adelaide, but there's now a Patrick Junior; that's him, sitting on my wife's lap.'

'Good God almighty, how about that!' a shocked Manfred replied.

'Bugger the fence, let's have that brew you were talking about. And for God's sake man, get your lovely lady and your boy over here; it seems we've got heaps to talk about, eh?

'I must say though, Harry, you're looking as strong as ever and if I'm not mistaken, they're the same Walers you had last time we met.'

Harry waved to Jane who then, leading the packhorse and Harry's mount, walked the horses over to the men. Harry took Patrick Junior from Jane and even after she had dismounted, the boy clung shyly to his father.

Bluey and Manfred were immediately introduced to Jane. Both were obviously taken by her beauty and by her confident, yet disarming manner. 'It's nice to meet you gentlemen. I recall Harry talking about you two and your exploits. I do hope we're not disturbing your normal goings-on.'

'If by *goings-on* you mean cattle duffing,' Manfred replied seriously, 'well, you'd be wrong. This property is now ours and the cattle you see over there are also ours; with paperwork to prove it.'

'Just joking boys,' Jane replied, 'the past stays in the past as far as I'm concerned.'

'I can't recall if you blokes are married,' Harry asked hastily, partly to change the subject.

'Yep, we're both married,' Bluey replied. 'Why?'

'Just as well, because I was wondering why two women would be riding this way, flat out like.'

With little apparent effort, both riders reined in their horses and dismounted in one smooth, effortless movement. Though puffing and clearly exhilarated, both women stared with bemusement upon the small gathering, not just because of the unexpected strangers, but because a small child was happily perched on Bluey's shoulders.

Bluey and Manfred wasted no time introducing their wives, Flo and Gabby, first to Harry and Jane, and then to Patrick Junior. The women took it in turns to nurse Patrick junior while plying him with endearments and asking him many questions which, it seemed, confused the boy.

But what captivated the boy most about these friendly women was their long and wavy, bright red hair. But what staggered them all, was the way he held Flo's hair then Gabby's, each time persistently pointed towards Bluey: he'd somehow correctly reasoned that Flo and Gabby were sisters!

The newfound friends were all soon chatting happily without reservation or inhibitions, until Harry said, 'thanks for the brew, but let's get this fence fixed. It should only take an hour by the look of it; besides you don't want your cattle walking off during the night, eh.'

'Hey girls, why not take Jane and the nipper back to our place, Manfred suggested, 'you can get dinner on the go while we finish up here.'

Manfred spectacularly caught the mug his wife flung at him, though that may not have been her intention. Bluey, however, was not so lucky; he never saw the mug his wife launched at him, though he laughed good naturedly after it ricocheted off his shoulder, splattering its dregs over the side of his face.

42

———

What Harry and Jane initially had in mind would be just a few days stopover; somehow that estimate easily stretched to a companionable and productive three months.

The house was large and expansive and showing its age, but nevertheless easily accommodated its guests.

Furniture and bedding too, had seen better days, but did not lack comfort. The Coolgardie food safe was functional and the kitchen table, though randomly scored and notched was a very solid and stable piece which easily sat eight adults.

However, the flooring was another matter; the kitchen, and in particular the outside porch floorboards, had conceded not only to foot traffic and the weather, but to white ants.

Harry, Bluey and Manfred laboured hard, repairing and replacing kangaroo damaged fencing and rebuilding the stock yards. Their horses were a priceless asset, hauling freshly cut timbers either singly, or in tandem when a heavy corner post required more muscle.

The women too, each collected several blisters; their tasks ranged from expanding, tending and installing shade and bird deterrent coverings for the vegetable garden, to house cleaning and helping the men to replace several rotten internal and external floorboards. None complained and they could often be heard singing popular countrified songs either individually or in lilting harmony.

Many other jobs were shared. The long drop toilet was relocated further from the house, and several shade trees were planted adjacent to the new stockyards and nearby the house.

But the job that Jane liked most was finishing the underground cellar left by the previous property owners. Its entrance had been boarded over and easily removed, but a team effort was then needed to evict two rather upset tiger snakes before she could proceed with replacing the original shoring timbers and extending the cellar's length.

Harry was in his element alongside Jane as they wrangled the new support timbers into place and once that was completed, they happily set about fashioning and installing rows of red gum shelving. Though it was difficult and often frustrating to work in partial darkness, there was the very real benefit of it being several degrees cooler below ground.

Harry also had his own private project to complete… which had nothing to do with his fictitious explanation that it was "for extending the water tank platform to support either more, or larger tanks for the future."

Patrick Junior was spoilt rotten. Even if he evaded six pairs of adult eyes, it was comforting to know that on most occasions he could usually be found chatting non-stop with Bluey.

* * *

DAYLIGHT HOURS WERE NOW LESSENING, and each day dawned colder than its predecessor.

Harry, usually contented with each purposeful day, was feeling restless, a condition not so easily hidden from Jane. 'What say we make tracks, Harry?' Jane whispered while they lay, naked bodies entwined, unable to sleep.

'Again, my gorgeous girl, you've read my mind. We don't want to overstay our welcome, eh? Mind you it's been an amazing time and I reckon we've made friends who we'll never forget. I'll miss 'em; you too?'

'Of course, but not that much so long as I've got you and our gorgeous little man with us.'

The following day, Harry announced their intention to move on. The response from their hosts was one not only of surprise, but of deep sadness, even distress. Whilst Flo and Gabby fought back tears, Bluey and Manfred stared at each other in resignation.

Manfred was the first to respond. 'You don't *have* to leave you know; you're welcome to stay as long as you choose.'

'We know that Manfred, and we thank you,' said Jane, 'but we'll never get to Melbourne at this rate. But we'll never forget all of you, or the wonderful time we've had living here. We're friends forever, eh?'

Late the next morning, having packed their few belongings onto their pack horse and saddled their horses, it was time for the small family to leave.

While the women engaged in their own private farewell of hugs, kisses and tears, Harry said sombrely to Bluey and Manfred, 'I reckon we've all been lucky, eh? To think that you two had been nothing but common bushrangers, like, and how we met and how the both of you silly buggers got involved with that halfwit, Mad Dan Morgan. However, knowing what I do now, it's no surprise that we've become such good mates; and you two now being beef barons, like, eh?'

Handshakes and back slaps followed, then Harry and Jane mounted their impatient Walers. As Harry was about to wheel his horse to follow Jane, he called back to his friends. 'Look in the cellar, we've left you each a small gift and something a bit handier. Use 'em wisely.'

Patrick Junior saw but understood none of this parting ritual but had just enough awareness to wave both his hands before falling fast asleep.

As the three riders disappeared into the haze of the noonday sun,

Bluey emerged from the cellar carrying a small box and the mariner's telescope Patrick had given to Harry when he and Maddy left Echuca.

As Bluey's eyes adjusted to the glare outside the cellar, to his amazement the box contained four equal sized nuggets of gold. With equal surprise he then noticed what appeared to be a note, neatly folded and placed flat on the bottom of the box. Spreading the sheet of paper, he read:

My so-called tank stand extension will be a perfect platform from which to keep an eye on your boundary fences, eh?
And remember, it takes a thief to spot a thief.
Good luck for the future.
H and J and Patrick Junior. xxx

43

———————

In his private moments, ever since the *Sylphide* navigated its way to Melbourne, Harry often recalled his persistent fascination with the raw beauty and deadly reputation of Australia's southern coastline.

Perhaps it was that fascination that instinctively first led Harry west, away from the mighty Murray River and then south into the Mallee region. Though Harry and Jane relied for directions upon well intentioned locals, little did they know that the Mallee was the hottest and driest region in Victoria.

They were soon to discover that the Mallee was, for all practical purposes, completely flat and very low-lying, and, that most of the Mallee consisted of sand hills. Mallee eucalypts dominated what vegetation existed, though there was the occasional swamp with stands of casuarina.

Most of their travelling was done in the early daylight hours when they could not only savour the fresh, cool morning air, varied birdsong and the herbaceous, spicy fragrances of the desert... but the *awesome* affects upon the surrounding landscape as the rising sun immersed it in wondrous veils of blue, gold and mauve.

Huge eagles were also seen at their best in the morning as the earth warmed and the resultant updrafts took them soaring in search of food.

Nevertheless, as grand as that time was, nothing could beat the incredible Mallee sunsets. Immediately following their evening meal, in that time of peace and tranquillity after the flies had retired for the day and before the mosquitoes launched their night attacks, Harry, Jane and Patrick Junior would sit side-by-side in the sand and marvel at the magnificent display of colours generated by the sun as it retired below the western horizon. Even the horses seemed impressed; curtailing their foraging then standing motionless with heads raised, gazing into the west.

However, because the groundwater was highly saline, Harry and Jane soon realised their underestimation of the Mallee's dryness, being forced to impose upon wheat and barley farmers for fresh tank water. Most farmers were sympathetic and generous; others were not so caring or helpful.

At the first opportunity, six new canvas water bags were purchased, filled and then distributed between all three horses. This extra weight meant that Harry, Jane and Patrick Junior spent more time walking. It was during those times when many and different types of reptiles were observed. And birds; for there were hawks, hundreds of wrens with lilac breasts and long vertically held tail feathers, noisy multicoloured parrots and occasionally groups of eagles tearing apart the carcass of a hapless wallaby or kangaroo.

To *exercise* his shotgun, as Harry would say (*and not to stretch its barrel*, as Jane would counter), Harry regularly investigated what looked like a swampy area for he had learnt that such places often attracted bronze winged pigeons, ducks, snipe and even the occasional Mallee fowl: all fine eating fare.

He also learnt that most birds only approached these remote water holes at days end, so he became accustomed to patiently waiting beneath the cover of any nearby vegetation until the birds began to arrive.

Resisting the urge to brush away thirsty flies from the corners of his eyes and from within his nose was a taxing challenge, but he knew that any sudden movement would deny him of the one and only shot his shotgun would permit. Although Harry had become skilful at breaking the gun's breach, dropping his small pocketknife down the barrel to dislodge the spent cartridge and then reloading, it was generally a pointless operation, because by then, all potential targets had either scattered out of sight or were well out of range.

Nevertheless, Harry was a very good shot. And, on most occasions, providing his stealthy approach to the water hole remained undetected, his efforts were usually rewarded with multiple kills.

Another bonus was the water quality of the swamps, which occasionally proved to be sweet, or only slightly brackish, which, for practical reasons Harry always took a couple of empty water bags with him.

By now, Harry and Jane were teaching Patrick Junior how to pluck a dead bird's feathers and then remove its innards. This bored Patrick Junior, though strangely he was intrigued with their eyes; either prodding them with a stick or pressing at them with his chubby fingers.

As the miles and days slipped by, it was not uncommon to encounter Aboriginal families, usually when they were least expected. Though no threat or malice was displayed, they would not acknowledge Harry's and Jane's waving to them, beckoning them to stop for a yarn.

Oddly however, that always changed when Jane and Harry, with Patrick Junior perched upon his father's shoulders, chose to walk and lead their horses to give them some relief. Such encounters, though usually guarded at first would often develop into hospitable water sharing meetings.

Nevertheless, it was difficult to fully understand each other's attempts at meaningful dialogue. But when those aboriginal families had children in tow, Patrick Junior had no problem imposing himself upon them and joining in their games of throwing sticks in the hope of hitting almost impossible targets.

On only one occasion did Harry and Jane succeed in convincing an Aboriginal family to stay with them overnight at their camp. Little could be shared, until Harry, accompanied by Patrick Junior, two older Black men and three children located a small mob of kangaroos. Harry's only shot was true and nobody went hungry that night. But alas, the next morning, much to Patrick Junior's frustration the small family mob had vanished.

Harry and Jane were to later learn that these folk were *Wergaia* people, which meant people belonging to the Mallee. They were also known as the *Maligundidi*.

* * *

'Jane, my darling, I don't know how you keep the boy so clean; and the meals you concoct, well, they're always so damn good.'

'Yeah, it's a challenge alright, but I couldn't do it without you. You've no idea how much your help means to me while I'm getting meals ready or washing his lordship's clothes for instance. And I really do appreciate that you keep him busy showing him the critters that surround us and nursing him and telling him stories when I need to get to the toilet.

'But mind you, Harry dear, you could do better by tubbing up before we have dinner. And your socks could certainly do with a good drink occasionally!'

44

Gradually, as they trekked further south, the harshness of the Mallee gave way to a more open, undulating and fertile landscape known as the Wimmera region of western Victoria.

Improved roads assisted their progress, though the emergence of very early models of motorised vehicles—seldom previously encountered—became a challenge, particularly when their drivers persisted in honking their horns as they noisily rumbled by. Though their intentions were basically friendly, most drivers had little understanding of how long it took Harry and Jane to thereafter pacify their startled horses. Surprisingly, none of those drivers stopped to seek clarification of Harry's colourful and often impossible suggestions.

Vast paddocks of wheat and barley were complimented by flocks of sheep, dairy cows and beef cattle all grazing on lush, long green grass. The Grampians, a large mountain range with jagged peaks, loomed far to the east.

Eventually, they came upon a small freehold farm named *Karibeal*. All three were immediately made most welcome. The ageing owners, Lloyd and Doreen Downards, were second generation farmers, a devoted married couple about to test the possibility of selling their property since none of their four offspring showed any interest in carrying forward the family farming tradition.

A casual "just going by" meeting, intending to be only a chat and the possibility of a cuppa, resulted in an invitation to stay for as long they wished, for there were any amount of spare rooms. A strong rapport soon followed.

Over the following few weeks Harry took on most of the jobs normally reserved for Lloyd, while Jane threw herself into the house-work and learnt many new delicious and healthy recipes from Doreen. And it wasn't long before Jane was singing on top note, along with Doreen, or laughing at one of Doreen's witticisms.

As for Patrick Junior, he really took to Doreen's grandmotherly and scholarly demeanour and spent hours with her being tutored in the arts of writing and reading.

Yet, equally, he enjoyed being in Lloyd's company, either helping to pick fruit, feeding the chooks and collecting eggs, feeding the pigs, carrying armloads of firewood into the kitchen or shaping flat pieces of wood into cricket bats.

Often, following dinner, the four new friends would sit on the vine-laced front veranda and talk for hours. It was on one such occasion, that for some unexpected reason, the conversation shifted to discussing the Downards' predecessors.

Doreen quietly excused herself and left the veranda, soon though returning armed with a large folder bursting with family memorabilia. Slowly, she leafed her way through the folder's contents and suddenly murmured, 'Ah yes, here it is.'

"It" turned out to be a four-page typed letter with a centrally positioned heading ["Karibeal"] and a conventionally positioned Addressee ["Penyabyr. No 1."]. The letter was written by Doreen's great-grandfather, Elijah Houghton, directed to his (unnamed) brothers and sisters. It is also dated thus... *July the 7th 1880.*

"'Penyabyr'", Lloyd explained, 'is another small region or Parish, between Karibeal and the nearby Victoria Valley, about fifteen miles from here.'

'The "No. 1" is probably the number assigned to Elijah's family,'

Doreen suggested, 'and it was painted boldly on the side of a makeshift roadside letter box. But now it's a "pigeon-hole number" within a dedicated room attached to a nearby homestead. The owners volunteer a rudimentary mail service for the surrounding farmers, including us. Good neighbours, indeed. *Karibeal* is also the name they gave to their farm.

'Elijah's letter tells his family in England,' Doreen continued, 'about an apparent encounter with some justifiably angry aborigines near to where he was then working in South Australia.'

'We don't know where the *original* hand-written letter is,' Lloyd added, 'but for some reason a family member, prior to immigrating to Australia, took it upon themselves to transcribe and type it for posterity and presumably, for ease of circulating the letter to their "Colonial" relatives. One can only assume that the person who transcribed the letter was one of Elijah's brothers or, more likely, one of his sisters.'

'Here, Harry, read this,' said Doreen as she handed the letter to him. 'Make sure you read it too, Jane, I think you'll both find it rather interesting.

What they read, warts and all, was as follows: -

KARIBEAL
Penyabyr. No 1.
July the 7 1880

To My Dear Brothers and Sisters,
I promised you in my letters that I should send you an account of one of my adventures in South Australia for I have been a great traveller in this country and if you take as much pleasure in reading these lines as I take in writing them, we shall all be satisfied.

I shall begin with 24 hours adventures I had with the blacks in the big desert of South Australia. It was about 1863 that I took a situation as boundary rider on a sheep station in South Australia at a salary of £60 pounds per year with rations (when they found us). We had been there about three weeks when I thought I would go out in the desert and have a hunt after some wild cattle. So, putting my saddle on my horse away I started for a large sand hill about ten miles in the desert.

After going about seven miles I came across the tracks of a mob. I followed it for about 8 miles before I came up with them. I then singled out one about 2 years old. I chased it for a mile or two then I gave it a shot but missed it the bull turned on me and before I could get my horse out of his way, he had thrown me and my horse completely over end in the scuffle that ensued, my horse broke away and left me some 20 miles in the desert.

I had no fear on his account as I knew he would go to the Paddock gate that I had come through some 12 miles back.

By this time the day was getting far advanced and as I knew I could not get back to my hut that day I thought I would have a spell for a short time and then have a look round for a place to camp for the night. After resting myself for about one hour, I thought I would go to a rise about half a mile off and see what was beyond, and well was it that I did for in the hollow below, not greater than 300 yards from where I then stood, was a whole camp of wild blacks mustering at the least some 200 yards.

I now began to think that I was in a fair position for getting speared for I knew if they once saw me while it was light nothing would save me from their spears.

There happened to be some low branches not far off so I thought I might as well get under them till dark. I had not been under them more than five minutes when I saw a blackfellow on his hands and knees a following on the track that I had made with my boots. He was coming straight for the bush that I was in.

I let him come within about ten yards. I then began to think it was time for me to get ready for him so putting my gun through a opening in the bush I must have made a noise for he stopped and looked at the bush that I was in for about half one minute. He then crawled behind a bush about 20 yards from where I was. He then send one of his spears at me but it did me no harm but before he could throw another I was out of my bush and after his.

I should have shot him but I knew that the report of my gun would bring the whole tribe down upon me before I had time to put my distance between them and me.

By this time it was sundown and by the noise I heard over the hill I knew the black had got in camp. It was now a race for life as I knew concealment for the next half hour was no use as it would be too light so I started back in the direction that I had come.

I had not gone far when I heard them a coming over the sand hill not more than half a mile behind me. Dear brother if you had seen me run for life it would have done you good for I kept the same distance for about two miles and by this time it was pretty well dark and as I was tired a going at that pace I though I would plant under some low branches that I was passing at the time, so crawled under one. I waited to see whether they would pass by the bush or not, a few minutes would tell me as they were coming very fust but it was quite dark and I knew they could not see my tracks, they came within a few yards of the bush that I was in then disappeared in the dark beyond.

I kept in the bush for about one hour and as I was on the point of making another start I observed a fire arise not more than one hundred yards from the bush that I was in. I kept very quiet now for I knew that was a signal for them all to muster and see whether any of them had passed any signs of my trail. I could tell by the noise that they were making that they were coming in fast. I kept concealed for about one hour then I thought I would try to see what they were doing so leaving the bush I crawled to another that was not more than twenty yards from where they were camped and now Brother to give you an idea of a blacks camp sixteen years ago it would baffle description.

Fancy yourself in a vast desert surrounded on all sides with great plains with here and there a few low bushes with not a single white man within 30 miles and a swarm of blacks not more than 20 yards from where you were hid waiting for the light so that they could get on your tracks and spear you before you could get out of the desert it was not a very enviable position to be in.

Fancy brother about one hundred large monkeys sitting around a camp fire with half their bodies painted white, the other red some in the shape of a skeleton and in fact all colours and you have some idea of what a camp of wild blacks are in this country.

While I was looking the chief arose to make a speech and by his gestures he did not seem to be in a good temper. By and by he sat down then another one arose and by his gestures he was making them believe that he knew the direction I had taken he was causing quite a commotion in the camp and I was so eager to see them leaping around their camp fire that I had not thought to put down the hammer of my gun and in the excitement my gun went off, to see them all fall flat on their faces as if they were shot, so frightened were they at the report of my gun that it was a thing to see and never be forgot.

I waited about two hours from daylight. You may be sure I did not stay after this. I now made another start in the direction that I knew the station should be in. I had not gone more than 300 yards when the blacks recovered from their surprise and with one loud yell they started in pursuit. For about one mile they came straight behind me as if they could see me before them although it was very dark at this time but gradually their sounds died away then I knew they were at a loss which way I had taken. I went for about 2 miles further and as I was sure that I was going in the right direction I thought I would stop in some low bushes that I was passing at the time till daylight.

My first thought was to look for my gun for I knew they had not given up the persuit yet. I had not been in my concealment more than one hour when I could see that daylight was appearing, I made for a rise to see what direction I must take. I could tell by the country that I had about 8 miles to go before I was out of the desert.

I looked behind me to see whether they were a following me and to my horror I saw they had found my tracks and were not more than one mile behind me and as I went over the brow of the hill I could tell by the noise that they were making they had seen me.

It was now a long race of 8 miles as I knew they would follow as till I was out of the desert. It was down-hill for about 2 miles and I knew they could not gain on me while I was going down-hill but I was not so sure how it would be going up the next rise. I had run about one mile when I saw them coming over the rise behind. It was now a race for life as I knew if they got within 50 yards of me I should be speared for they could send their spears within a few inches of that distance and as I had given them a long race I knew they would not show me any mercy but I had fully made up my mind to use my gun upon them before they should become too close to use their spears.

I had now ran about three miles and was getting pretty well tired, the blacks had gained about a quarter of a mile by this time I could see them all now there were about 50 of them coming yelling with all their might by this time.

You might have heard me gasping 20 yards off for breath. I knew I could not hold out much longer and as there was a belt of scrub about one hundred yards further on I thought I would try to make for it then sell my life as dear as I could.

The blacks were now about 200 yards behind me, now I knew that another ten minutes would decide whether I should reach the timber or not. I had just got to the edge of the timber when they shot a whole shower of spears after me but I was just within the timber and got behind one big gum tree to wait for the first one that should show himself for I was fully determined to shoot him. After being behind the tree for about ten minutes I thought I would crawl to some more bushes that were about 2 yards further on. The blacks were stopping about 100 yards from where I was and they were yelling most frightenly a sure sign that they were really excited.

I knew that after they had taken a spell for a short time they would try and surround me so I thought I would make the most of my time so starting again I had not gone more than 300 yards when I came to the other side of the scrub and to my surprise there was the gate that I had come through the day before and what was better my horse was there waiting to be let through.

I soon had my horse by the bridle then I knew I was safe and had only just got on my horse when the blacks made one great rush at the tree that I had been behind a few minutes before. To hear their yels of disappointment as they saw me sit on my horse only 20 yards further on would baffle any description that I could give you. They saw that all hopes of catching me were gone and in an instant they let fly a whole shower of spears at me but I knew what their taticks would be so that I was prepared for them and rode about 50 yards further of them, I fired my gun in their direction, they ten vanished in the scrub and I saw no more of them at that time.

I now rode to my hut that was a few miles further on and I knew

Harriet would be in a great way on account of my long absence such is 24 hours I had in the desert with the blacks but I have had more than their spears flying around my head of which I will tell you another time so no more this time.

Your ever affectionate brother
Elijah Houghton.

'As you can see,' said Doreen as Patrick handed the letter to Jane, 'despite his many spelling mistakes and occasionally sloppy grammar, Elijah's letter is of a reasonable quality. He certainly wrote with *some* competence and passion and tells a good yarn, which indicates to me that he was well educated... a rarity of that era.

'Lloyd and I are neither totally convinced about his true intentions, nor of his integrity, so we'll leave it up to each of you to decide if Elijah's letter is true, or a tall story that promotes his overblown ego?'

* * *

WHEN JANE HANDED the letter back to Lloyd, she said in a thoughtful tone, 'There were several disturbing questions which arose in my mind.

'For example, apparently Elijah before leaving to seek work in South Australia, was not a very well-liked person either around Penyabyr, or in the Victoria Valley region.'

'That's absolutely right,' said Lloyd. 'We knew he was often arrogant and aloof. And why was Elijah, seemingly a well-educated and reasonably wealthy man, in such a position that he needed to take on additional work as a boundary rider?'

'What annoys me is,' Harry interrupted, 'if you substitute "a mob of cattle" for a "mob of aborigines", Elijah's story takes on a particularly sinister quality. Was he really following the tracks made by a mob of cattle, not the tracks of aborigines? And if the "bull" which he apparently shot at is replaced by "an aborigine," then his urgent escape story may indeed have *some* credibility.'

'And why,' added Lloyd, 'would Elijah want to shoot a single two-year-old wild bull? It's well known that the meat from a bull is far less flavoursome than that from either a steer or a heifer.'

[Regrettably, at that time in Australia's history, it was perceived by certain white settlers (from all around Australia) that they still had a common "right and custom to seek out and shoot aborigines... for "sport"!

That abhorrent and merciless practice was eventually stamped out, but ridiculous reminders celebrating the lives of those who perpetrated such atrocities still remain on display around Victoria to this day. For example, the monument celebrating Angus McMillan, who, though arguably a skilled, pioneering grazier, was also the patronising ringleader of a group who heartlessly and regularly murdered many innocent aborigines.]

'So you two,' Jane asked respectfully, 'did Elijah believe it was also "*his right* to follow some reprehensible custom of shooting aborigines for sport"?'

After a thoughtful pause, Doreen replied, 'You know what, Jane? There was a rumour, which still exists in this general region, that on his deathbed, Elijah boasted about murdering a Chinese gold digger "for little or no reason".

'So Jane, do *you* think he had an entrenched disregard for all aboriginal folk?' Doreen asked. 'I for one believe he did, given how he described them in such a condescending manner; and that deeply shames me.

'What say you, Harry?'

'Disregard is one thing, but believing because he was white, supposedly God fearing and an Englishman and that he therefore somehow had a right to murder black people, dishonours all of us... and *that's not on*!

'Doreen, I don't mean to offend you in any way. You've clearly not inherited any of his nature. But, if it were me, I'd send any memory of Elijah to hell where I'm sure his soul will reside for ever: I'd throw that bloody letter in the fire and forget he ever existed!'

45

A month later, leaving Harry and Jane to keep an eye on their farm, Lloyd and Doreen went to stay with some old friends and an elderly relative who lived in the Victoria Valley, about fifty miles away.

They had planned to spend at least a month away from the farm, but unexpectedly returned after only two weeks.

'While we get changed and freshen up, put the kettle on, Jane, there's a good girl. We've got some rather discomforting news to tell you. I do hope Patrick is having his sleep for we need some quiet adult time.'

'Strewth, it *does* sound important,' said Harry, 'but don't worry, we should be right. I put Patrick to bed about twenty minutes ago; he won't surface for another hour or so.

'I'll unload your buggy and put the horses in the house yard. I should give 'em a good wash and curry combing now, but I suppose that'll have to wait until we've finished our chat.'

Once they were all seated, Jane was the first to speak. 'Well, c'mon Doreen, what's got you so worked up?'

Doreen took a sip of her cuppa, took a deep breath, then said, 'do you recall the conversation we had a few weeks ago about Elijah; you know, about him supposedly being dead?

'Yes? Well, we now have it on very good authority that he's alive and living a hermit's life in the Victoria Valley! He's been seen a few times by our friends and others who recognised him; albeit he's now a stooped and nearly bald old man, though he's still apparently got some wisps of white hair left.'

'It would seem,' Lloyd chimed in, 'he was not ill in the sense that he had a life-threatening disease, but rather, that he's not quite the full quid; you know, like he's lost his marbles. Anyway, he *was* previously sent to Melbourne and placed in an asylum for his own safety and treatment. Apparently though, about three years ago, he just up and walked out... and God only knows how, but he found his way back to this region.'

'We have no idea how he's survived, either where he lives or if he'll ever return here to annoy us,' Doreen added, 'but we certainly don't want anything to do with him; relative or not!'

Lloyd continued in a much more serious tone. 'We've also been told he has a gun and that several farmers reckon the odd sheep or two of theirs mysteriously disappear from time to time.

'And those who reckon they've spoken with Elijah in the past few years, say he can speak coherently, but then without any prompting lapses into rolling his eyes and mumbling things like "you'll see, I'll get all those fucken blacks", or "there's no place here for them stinking black bastards". A most disconcerting tirade, you'll agree. It seems Elijah hasn't changed one iota, I'm afraid.'

* * *

'So my boy, would you like to have a dog or two?' Harry quizzed his son.

'Do you mean puppies, da?' replied a very excited Patrick. 'And would they really be mine?'

'I can't promise they'll be pups, son, but they will be yours. We need to get the right dogs and teach them to protect the farmhouse when we need to work out in the paddocks. We don't want bad men sneaking inside and stealing things from us, do we now? And mister and missus Downards are getting old and your dogs could look after them too.

'But regardless my boy, you'll have to promise you'll help your ma and da to feed them. So what do you reckon son?'

'Will they grow into big dogs, da?'

'Yes, but you'll grow to be much bigger than them and you should turn out to be good pals. I'm not sure when I can get them, but soon I hope.'

* * *

By an amazing stroke of good luck, Harry's wishes were answered in a most unexpected fashion. About two weeks later, a travelling bric-a-brac salesman arrived at the Karibeal farmhouse hoping to sell his wares. After rolling up the canvas sides of his covered wagon, he proudly displayed an amazingly varied and countless wealth of items.

New socks, underwear, shirts and shoelaces were high on Jane's priority list and Doreen bought a bolt of material to make shirts for Lloyd and herself. Foodstuffs were also available, tea, sugar, flour, spices, cheese and raspberry cordial were all most welcome; but alas, no butter. Lloyd got lucky; the salesman even had some ready rubbed tobacco and several packs of cigarette papers.

While Jane, Doreen and Patrick Junior carried their purchases inside to unpack and put the kettle on for a cuppa, Harry, Lloyd and the travelling salesman, Tim Blackler, lingered for a chat under the verandah. A jovial conversation ensued but somehow meandered on to the subject of working dogs.

Tim, a wily middle-aged man listened patiently as Harry outlined his desire to buy a suitable pair of watchdogs. 'Great minds think alike, Harry, I've been thinking of doing much the same and I've been keepin' me eyes and ears open, like.

'There's a bloke I know who lives in Harrow, a small settlement not more than twenty miles from here. God only knows why, but he's got about thirty dogs of just about every breed yah can imagine. If it were me, I'd pay him a visit and see if he can help yah. Here, I'll write down his name, so you won't forget. Should you see him, tell him I recommended him; there might be a bob or two in it for me, if yah know what I mean. His name's Jock, Jock Beebe; you won't find a nicer bloke.'

46

With the promise that they would return within a few days and that Doreen and Lloyd would take good care of him during his parent's brief absence, Patrick Junior accepted his lot with amazingly good temper.

* * *

HARROW WAS a typical one street country settlement. It comprised of a farrier's workshop and an adjoining wheelwright fabricator's yard on one side and a general produce come hardware store on the other. At the very end of the main street, only sixty yards or so long, stood a huge peppercorn tree which threw its substantial cloak of shade across the roofs of the only hotel and the adjacent butcher's shop.

Yet strangely, the other few shops were bereft of decent shade.

A small creek ran behind the hotel, on both sides of which grew towering redgum eucalypts with vast shade canopies. A few red cattle and recently shorn sheep grazed peacefully beneath those trees... until a flock of sulphur crested cockatoos shrieked their disapproval at Harry's and Jane's intrusion and sending those animals off in a totally unnecessary, short-lived stampede.

The owner of the Harrow hotel happily gave directions to "Jock the dogman's house," which he euphemistically referred to as a *recluse's paradise.*

There could be no mistaking they had found the right place, for after riding a mile or so along a well-defined dirt road that threaded its way between thick scrub and further stands of tall eucalypts, they eventually entered a clearing, enclosed as far as they could see in both directions by hand hewn post and rail fencing.

To the south, about fifty yards away, stood a dilapidated farmhouse which immediately offended Jane's senses to see a house surrounded by what could only be described as rubbish. Equally, Harry wondered how this chap could possibly find anything useful in such a collection of waste and cast-off bits and pieces.

And they were most definitely *not* alone! An incredible cacophony of barking dogs had announced their arrival and maintained their boisterous welcome. All were chained to their kennels, in most cases simply a hollow log each positioned far enough from one other to prevent physical contact, no matter how hard or violently they pulled on their chains.

Both horses initially jinked in fright and although they remained skittish, were patiently brought under control. Ignoring the ongoing uproar, Harry and Jane urged their horses towards the house where they dismounted to the sounds of creaking saddle leather.

The back door opened slowly with a rasping reluctance, obviously requiring considerable effort by someone inside, due to either swollen or misaligned floorboards, or a sagging door, or most likely, both.

Eventually, a tall, well-groomed gentleman emerged. 'Greetings friends, lovely to see you, but what on earth brings you to my humble abode? Please ignore the dogs, they're impatient for their evening meal: a bit early yet; but they'll not bother you.'

Most unexpectedly, Jock suddenly looked away from his visitors and yelled on top note, 'will you lot please shut up; can't you see I've got guests?' Uncannily, the racket abruptly lessened, then stopped.

'G'day Mr Beebe, *that* was pretty damn clever,' Jane responded in her most charming voice, before commencing her formal introductions. 'My name's Jane and this is my husband, Harry Taylor. A mutual friend, Mr Tim Blackler, recommended we seek you out for we have great need for a couple of guard dogs... pets for our son in the first instance, but essentially dogs which will not just threaten, but attack on command any unwanted intruders.'

'And knowing Tim,' replied Jock as he shook hands with Harry, 'he'll no doubt be after a monetary commission, but first things first. I think you've come to the right place, so please make yourselves comfortable and tell me more precisely what you have in mind. No promises though, most of my pack are mature animals and set in their ways.'

* * *

'I'D NEVER HAVE BELIEVED we'd even fluke getting such a deal,' said Harry happily as they set off for home. 'So what say you, girl? Are you totally pleased with the intended additions to our family? Mainly though, do you see *any risk* that Patrick might get set upon by the dogs we've chosen, like?'

'My darling Harry, if I had any doubts we'd not be having this chat. So come on, shake a leg, I can't wait to give our beautiful boy a big hug. Play your cards right mister and you just might get lucky too.'

* * *

AT THE AGREED day and time, Jock arrived at the Downards property driving an open topped buggy. Accompanying him were two grand looking dogs, one perched on either side of Jock on the driver's seat.

As Harry tied the horse's reins to the front fence, Jock called his greeting. 'G'day you two; great to see you again and this must be young Patrick if I'm not mistaken? And these two grinning clowns accompanying me are Peggy and Fruitmince.

'As you can see, they're not the two I was going to sell you but give me a chance and after dinner I'll explain their attributes and therefore, why I overlooked the one's you initially wanted to buy. Mind you, there will be no price change.

'Peggy here's the proud mother of this young bloke; she's about three years old, and he's from her first litter. I call him Fruitmince because I have no idea who his sire is, yet he seems to have a bit of everything in him. Still, he's a promising type as you'll soon discover. And according to my records, he's about eleven months old.'

'Please, come inside Jock and I'll introduce you to Doreen and Lloyd Downards. They own this lovely property and they're getting on a bit, but I reckon you'll like them,' Jane chimed in, 'I'll put the kettle on and show you to your room while Patrick gives you a hand with your things. Harry'll put your horse and the buggy in that shed, over there. There's plenty of good feed and water inside and your horse can move around freely after Harry unhitches it.'

'Very kind of you Jane, but Harry, if it were me,' said Jock with a glint of warning in his eyes, 'I'd leave these two brutes tied up in the buggy for a while, just to settle in, like. There's no knowing whether they'll take a shine to you straight away; let's just hope they don't insist on showing you their rather large, beautiful teeth.

'Anyway Harry, we start their training tonight. I want you and your boy to feed them after we've had our dinner. It's important you reinforce upon them that they get fed only once a day, only at days end and only ever by either you, or young Patrick. That can't be Jane's job, even if Harry's late getting home from the paddocks.

* * *

As nature would have it, Patrick Junior's innocence seemed to captivate both dogs who were soon all over him, both vying to either lick his face, or to gently hold his tiny hands in their mouths. Patrick's smiles and laughter were contagious, but no less genuinely than his parent's obvious relief, particularly when neither animal retaliated as Patrick playfully tried to push them away. Jock too, seemed mightily pleased.

'Dunno how you've done it Harry,' Jock later confided, 'but both dogs accept your company and obviously relish your authority; they wouldn't be so willing to come to you, otherwise. But from tomorrow they must begin to understand the reason for them being here.

'Over the next two weeks or so Harry, I may at times seem to be a bit harsh with them and you, but if you want guard dogs who will only attack on your signal, then that's how it must be. I'll do my level best with them, but I can assure you that in thirty years of training all sorts of working dogs, these two have, in my estimation, the greatest temperament and natural abilities. You'll see that soon enough.

'You're already bonding with them beautifully, Harry, but we can't be fooled by their good nature. During their initial training, some things might set them off and it's my job to see to it that no matter what young Patrick might do to them, they will not harm him, or Jane... or you, for that matter.

'But make no mistake, Harry, they *will* be different dogs after their training because they must learn to attack *only on your command*... a disposition they'll take to their graves to protect not only you, but Jane and young Patrick of course.'

47

ABOUT SIX MONTHS LATER

Despite whispers circulating about complaints made by local aborigines that they were being needlessly harassed by a person, or persons unknown, this was not foremost in Harry's mind as he rode solo to a particularly beautiful region to the west of Harrow, a place of lush pasture, undulating hills and deep valleys.

His senses were at peace afforded by the companionship of his trusted Waler and his dogs and not focused upon recent disturbing news that someone had been rolling rocks down those valleys upon a mob of innocent aborigines.

At the crest of one such valley, Harry reined in his Waler and signalled to his dogs to "stay back," because movement below had caught his eye and he had smelt a hint of smoke upon the breeze that gently drifted up from the valley.

The movement Harry saw was that of an ageing aboriginal man making haste to a thicket of scrub, no doubt intent upon answering an urgent call of nature.

The Waler nodded its head and whinnied softly. Both dogs were obediently sitting side by side but growling with menace, for they too had clearly seen the old man, though in reality they sensed he was no threat to their master.

Suddenly however, both dogs stood, ears pricked and their growls far more serious, for they had just seen something else far more threatening. Seconds later, Harry too was focusing on the cause of their agitation. 'Sit!' he hissed. Begrudgingly, both dogs resumed sitting but they were now trembling; anticipating action yet daring not to disobey Harry's command.

Harry dismounted and stood behind his dogs. He could now clearly see another man, a white man no less with receding white hair who was shuffling forward, hunched over and carrying a rifle... and almost at a vantage point about twenty yards above where the old black man had taken up a position within a small thicket of scrub and was now intent on voiding his bowels.

Seconds later a shot rang out. The old black man clutched at his chest as he fell forward, then twitched violently in his death throes.

'Attack!' Harry instantly yelled, an almost needless command to his dogs as he swung up and onto his Waler. 'Just wait till I get my hands on you, you rotten murdering bastard!'

There was no second shot. However, there were agonising screams aplenty as Peggy and Fruitmince tore into the white man, savaging his exposed neck, shoulders, and arms.

As he arrived at the scene, Harry was horrified by the wounds inflicted upon the shooter. Nothing of surgical precision, just torn and peeled-back skin, exposed sinews and ripped muscle tissue: so much carnage for just a few brief seconds since his dogs had attacked!

'Release!' Harry yelled. Peggy immediately responded.

'You too Fruitmince! Release and stand! Now, or I'll sink my boot so far up your arse you'll go cross-eyed!'

Fruitmince however, before relenting, again sunk his teeth deep into the man's flabby, unprotected side and then viciously shook his powerful head from side to side.

Almost as an afterthought, Fruitmince released the man and

stepped back proudly as if surveying his handywork. He then retreated, snarling with rage, or was it just youthful excitement?

Though bleeding copiously and still clutching his rifle, the man mumbled, almost incoherently, 'Got the blackie, eh? Dead as a tur...' But before he could finish, Harry ripped the rifle from the murderer's grip and silenced him with a savage kick to the side of his head.

Still shuddering with uncontrolled rage, Harry put the barrel of his shotgun to the man's head. But by the Grace of God perhaps, just before he pulled the trigger, a waft of sanity intervened to clear his head.

Abruptly, through his now receding rage, it registered with him that his dogs were again growling their most serious warnings from somewhere behind him. Harry froze. However, sensing a real danger, he turned... slowly.

Before him were eleven black men, all armed and all clearly very angry. Peggy and Fruitmince however, standing firm between both parties, suddenly adopted a most threatening attitude; hackles raised, ears back, lips raised to expose their huge fangs and their snarls somewhere between coughing and full-throated barking.

'Alright you two. Good dogs. Now, *'back off and sit!'*

To Harry's surprise and enormous relief, all of the black men also took several steps back and while so doing, lowered their weapons. In return, Harry placed his shotgun on the ground.

An elder, perhaps fifty years old, stepped forward and said in easily discernable English, 'what you want tah do wid dat fella? I reckon him dead. No good white fella, 'im should go tah hell.'

'I'm really so sorry for your loss,' Harry pleaded. 'That bloke, he should not have murdered this old man; he very bad fella alright. Sick in his head. This should not have happened. I tried to stop him but was too damn late; I'm sorry.

'He'll go to hell for sure, but I can't take his body with me. What do your mob want to do?'

'Maybe dingoes not even want to eat him. But we get rid of him, alright? No one evah see him again. You nevah talk of this? And we nevah say nothin' 'bout dis. So you must go now.'

Harry then stepped forward and shook the black man's hand; his return grip was firm and he looked Harry square in the eyes, their mutual understanding acknowledged without a further word being uttered.

As Harry and his dogs crested the summit of the gully, he turned in his saddle intending to wave farewell to his co-conspirators, but there was no sign of them, or of their dead elder, or of the now probably dead white man. However, about that last person, Harry was wrong: a faint, agonising scream rose from the valley floor, faded and then suddenly stopped.

What Harry now correctly guessed was that the scoundrel Elijah Houghton, *was* finally dead and that Doreen and Lloyd need no longer fear his possible invasion of their peaceful lives.

48

———————

arry elected to return home via a different route for no reason other than it might offer a change of scenery.

For most of the time, Harry allowed his Waler to lope along at a sedate canter. Peggy and Fruitmince, tongues hanging out, but not breathing heavily, ran easily without altering their own pace, one on each side of the Waler.

Miles upon miles of lush, green, undulating country, interspersed with huge, ancient redgums spread before them as far as Harry could see, filling the air with a fresh, clean, eucalypt fragrance.

The occasional mob of kangaroos confronted them, some standing at their full height to satisfy their curiosity before bounding away. Others continued grazing as if nothing concerned them.

Though both dogs showed their interest in the roos, a quiet, but authoritative 'no,' quickly quashed any ideas of a sporting chase.

Harry admired the occasional opulent, Edwardian designed, bluestone homestead which dominated the landscape and wondered where the materials and tradesman had come from to build such grand buildings.

Without warning while lost in his thoughts, suddenly Harry

received two uninvited realisations. First, how was he going to break his news about Elijah and second, he had concluded it was time to find his own family home... probably in Melbourne where he could guarantee a first-class education for his son.

* * *

WHILE IN THAT MEDITATIVE STATE, Harry's thoughts turned to his great friend, Patrick. He missed Patrick's relaxed, intelligent, reliable and adventurous company. 'We must catch up soon, rather than later,' he mused. '"The tyranny of distance" might be real, but wake up Harry, that's no excuse.'

Via letter swapping, Harry knew Patrick was safe and still dearly loved his wife, Maddy and their son, Stanley.

He also knew that Patrick had his own boat building business, a sixty-acre small farming property, a beautiful house with an ocean view at Largs Bay, a motor vehicle and three horses. And, that despite his age, had been recruited by The Australian Navy to oversee the fit-out of a Merchant ship for the transportation of Australian horses to South Africa, should the British need military support in their endeavours against the fanatical Boer forces operating against British interests.

Harry acknowledged all of that enterprise was well and good, but not the same as learning about it while being in one another's company, albeit if it was only for a short time.

What neither Harry nor Patrick knew was that Teddy Green, after his arrival at Echuca and learning that his quarry had parted company, had come to the realisation that it would be futile to pursue Patrick down river. However, because Teddy also knew with a high degree of certainty that Harry was in Victoria... Harry would now become his *singular focus*!

* * *

Upon Harry's return to the Downards property, Doreen and Lloyd were obviously relieved he had arrived home unscathed. However, their relief was indifferent toward their relative, Elijah, who could no longer threaten anyone... and made an excellent show of not revealing the true depth of their relief.

Jane too was relieved her man was safe. Of Elijah, she secretly didn't give a damn, while Patrick Junior fussed over *his* dogs and insisted upon his da telling him (many times over) how brave they had just been.

Of Harry's announcement that it was time for his family to move on, Patrick Junior was distraught, but succumbed to accepting his parent's decision when his da changed his mind and agreed that his dogs could accompany them to Melbourne.

Doreen and Lloyd were at first shocked and saddened that their young friends, now considered family, would be leaving, but were also understanding and pragmatic because they had finally decided to retire and to live in Melbourne.

These lovely folk, who to Jane and Harry were their other mum and dad, would not accept payment for providing a roof over their heads. Nor could Doreen and Lloyd fully understand why Harry did not make an offer to buy their property until he explained that it was his duty to see his son receive the best possible formal education.

With significant "know how" from a trusted local real estate agent, Harry and Jane helped to find a buyer for the Downards property. An enthusiastic Adelaide investor swooped upon the beautiful land and home package, offering a handsome price to secure the deal.

* * *

Despite receiving wonderful care, Melbourne held little appeal for Doreen and Lloyd. Sadly, both passed away a year after their arrival at the retirement village; many said from broken hearts... that they so badly missed the peace and beauty of their family home.

* * *

JANE FOUND THEIR "IDEAL HOUSE" in the outer eastern suburbs of Melbourne; a bit too large for just the three of them, but that was soon to change for a second child was impatient to join the Taylor family.

49

———————

During the intervening three years, Teddy had meandered aimlessly throughout western Victoria in search of clues to help him locate his foe. Though most of his endeavours resulted in dead ends, he never lost his motivation and eventually got lucky at a pub in the small settlement of Harrow.

Following a now well-established routine, he sidled up to the only customer at the bar and amicably introduced himself. 'Edward Green's the name. Can I shout you a beer, mate?'

'Yeah, why not; thanks. Me name's Royce, Royce Latchford. Where you from, Edward? I haven't seen you about; new to the area are yah?'

'Nah, just passing through. I'm on the lookout for a suitable grazing property, or one to manage, perhaps,' Teddy lied, then purposefully took a deep gulp of his beer while hoping his lie sank in. 'I've also been looking for a mate of mine. I was told he lived around here.'

'If yah got deep pockets, there's some prime land up for grabs not far to the east of here. What's your mate's name? I might know him; I've lived here for nearly twenty years.'

'Harry, Harry Taylor... late twenties, strong looking lad, usually wears a full beard and about six foot tall. Do yah know him?'

'Can't say I do, sorry,' said Royce as he downed the last of his beer. 'Hang on a second. Come to think of it, I reckon our local dog breeder sold an animal or two to a bloke by that description; about ten or so months ago. He just might know where yah can find your friend. Nice bloke. His name's Jock. Say g'day to him for me will yah if yah catch up with him.

'Here, I'll draw you a map where you'll find Jock's house. But mind you, keep well away from his dogs.'

Suddenly breathless in surprise, the tickle of long overdue success snaked its way down Teddy's spine.

'Yeah, thanks, I'll do that, but look, I've gotta make tracks. Nice meeting you Royce.'

'What a dumb, know-all bastard,' Teddy arrogantly thought as he walked excitedly from the pub clutching Roy's crude but most useful map.

* * *

'YEAH, I KNOW THE LAD,' said Jock in response to Teddy's casual questioning. 'He was living at the Downards property, about fifty miles from here, but he and his family moved to Melbourne some time back.'

'So you don't know where he lives? Melbourne's a big place I understand.'

'Not *actually*, no. But we've kept in touch by letter. If you like, I'll get his Post Office box number. Hang on, I'll be back in a minute.'

While Jock searched inside his house for one of Harry's letters, Teddy fidgeted in his saddle, barely able to refrain from dismounting to give Jock *a bloody good hurry up.*

'Here you go, take this,' said Jock, 'the details are on the back of the envelope. That's the best I can do for you, mate. Good luck.'

'Much appreciated. I'll be on my way then. Good day to you, sir.'

'Another dumb shit,' Teddy thought to himself as he put his horse into a canter.

When out of sight from Jock's house and being pissed off by the incessant barking coming from Jock's dogs, Teddy dismounted, picked up a sizeable rock and threw it with all his strength into the midst of Jock's chained dogs.

Of course, he didn't achieve his desired result to silence them; quite the opposite, an unbelievable cacophony erupted, causing Teddy to quickly remount and urge his horse into a flat-out gallop away from the noise.

Regardless, Teddy Green didn't give a tinkers toss for he now knew how to find his archenemy; the imbecile who had stolen *his* gold. And he was certain a suitable bribe would do the trick to finally reveal Harry's residential address.

* * *

COINCIDENTALLY, far away at Largs Bay, Patrick was finalising a surprise visit to Melbourne for it was high time Maddy and Stanley should meet Harry's family.

50

———————

Harry and Patrick sat in the kitchen of the Taylor family house, elated and at last having some uninterrupted one-on-time time together, which the temporary absence of their respective wives and sons had so thoughtfully afforded them.

Jane and Maddy were at the far end of the house paddock, grooming and feeding Harry's horses after returning from a ride, a ride shortened by not wanting to risk harm to Jane because of her advanced pregnancy.

Stanley and Patrick Junior were in a nearby vacant block of land with some of their newfound friends, all happily trying to kick the leather from a hapless football.

The Taylors' kitchen was homely and functional. Polished wooden floors, two tastefully wallpapered walls, a double sink over which a window commanded a wide, outside view of not only the backyard but of the Dandenong Ranges, a food preparation bench, cupboard space taking up the fourth wall and a heavy-duty wooden table surrounded by six high backed chairs... and also on the fourth wall, in a place of obvious pride, was a single barrel shotgun supported by two brass brackets. The back door opened outwards onto the elevated back verandah, from which four steps descended to the back yard and a well-manicured lawn.

The two men were well into their second bottle of beer, occasionally laughing loudly as they reminisced, or in subdued, yet serious voices, expanded upon their respective future plans.

Totally unannounced, the kitchen's back door flew open. A man wielding a handgun hurled himself into the kitchen and immediately pointed his gun at Harry, then excitedly, turned it upon Patrick... then back again upon Harry.

The intruder was clearly down on his luck if the shabby state of his soiled and ill-fitting clothing and horrible body odour was any indication. But worse, he was obviously agitated, his grotesque snarl and wild-eyed expression barely hidden by his long and unkempt beard.

'Gotcha, yah bastards!' He shouted triumphantly. 'Stay seated and keep yah hands where I can see 'em, or else...'

'Or else what?' replied Harry, rapidly trying to compose himself against the shock invasion of his home.

'Try something stupid and you'll soon find out. Just remember, Taylor, you're a long time dead.'

'Right. But what exactly do you want, pray tell?' Patrick asked in his most non-confrontational tone.

'I want the gold you bastards stole from me. There's no way you could have spent it all, so hand it over! All of it! Now!'

'Hang on a minute,' Patrick interjected, 'You're Teddy, Teddy bloody Green!' But it can't be, you're dead! We both saw your horse kick you in the head.'

'Well, I'm not dead and it's my business to know how I survived, and up to you two dopes to wonder about forever.

'So, just give me *my gold* and I'll leave. And if you don't, I'll take great delight in killing both of you shits, right here and now... and then yah pox ridden wives and dumb clunk kids!'

'Listen, Teddy, we never had *your* gold, as you reckon it was. You must get it into your head that there *is no gold to be had!*' Harry lied, while observing Teddy's increasingly erratic posturing and knowing full well there was, albeit in a place only known to him and Jane.

'Look, Teddy, we have no axe to grind,' Patrick added, having quickly picked up on Harry's con hopefully to mentally disarm the deranged intruder. 'But seriously, like us, have you ever stopped and considered it possible that Clive may have been the recipient of all that stolen gold?'

Teddy stopped his impulsive wanderings: he'd taken the bait! Distracted, the gun dipped slightly in his hand. 'Nah, don't be so bloody stupid, that's utter bullshit, yah can't fool me!'

'But it's true, Teddy.' Patrick responded. 'We've got our own scuttle on Clive's devious interests.'

'Well, I've got me own proof, so stop wasting...,' were Teddy's last mutterings.

Oblivious to what was confronting their fathers, Stanley and Patrick Junior, laughing on top note and having vied to be first up the back steps, suddenly charged shoulder to shoulder through the back door and into the kitchen.

Startled, Teddy swivelled to challenge whoever it was had interrupted his plans, thereby unintentionally giving Harry and Patrick their first real chance to act.

As the kitchen door was in the process of closing, Patrick launched himself at the boys, bravely shoving them back onto the verandah and out of harm's way, demanding they run next door immediately. Teddy's first, albeit erratic, panicked shot, only just missed Patrick's head as he had dived to save the boys.

This distraction also gave Harry sufficient time to lunge from his seat and rip his shotgun from the wall and in one smooth action, cock its hammer.

But Harry need not have bothered; it just wasn't Teddy Green's Day.

Two blurs of fur, legs and angry gnashing fangs hit Teddy before he could protect himself. His second and final desperate shot also missed both dogs and Patrick, but nevertheless it punched a hole through the ceiling.

Fortuitously, given Fruitminces's bone crushing grip and relentless head shaking of Teddy's wrist, the gun fell from his hand; useless as it landed on the kitchen floor.

Only Harry had been aware that his dogs had come to investigate and stood quivering at the back door in anticipation of action. Both had immediately responded to his silent hand signal to "attack"... and did exactly as their training dictated.

Harry called his dogs off, then quickly kicked Teddy's gun across the floor and straight into Patrick's hands.

In despair, bleeding profusely from his multiple wounds and recognising that his long-awaited plan had just vapourised, somehow Teddy still managed to shoulder his way past the hands trying to refrain him. He then dashed from the back door, jumped down the four steps onto the lawn and ran for his life.

At that same time, Jane and Maddy, having heard the gun shots and fearing the worst, were running towards the house, unwittingly along Teddy's would be escape path.

'JANE! MADDY! GET DOWN!' Harry yelled as loud as he could while simultaneously shouldering his shotgun.

Luckily, understanding the urgency in Harry's cry, Jane grabbed Maddy's arm and tugged. 'Down, quick!' Jane yelled, her call matching Harry's plea.

'HOLD IT HARRY,' Patrick yelled, 'you can't shoot him, he's unarmed!'

'Oh, YES, I can! Nobody threatens my family and friends. Watch this.'

Harry's gun roared. Jane gasped and Maddy screamed as thirty or so lead pellets, impatient to seek their real target, "whooshed" by, only inches above their heads.

But Harry missed!

That hornet's nest of pellets struck the lawn, about twelve inches from Teddy's retreating backside. But Jane had had enough of this, gallantly throwing out her left leg which, just in time, succeeded in tripping Teddy.

Teddy stumbled, legs and arms windmilling madly, then fell flush on his face, causing him to again scream in pain. Gradually he raised himself onto his hands and knees, sobbing, because he now had to accept his fantasy was over.

Before he could stand, once again Peggy and Fruitmince were sent into action, commanded to place themselves either side of Teddy and to "stay"! To Teddy's horror, the dogs were again snarling ferociously, while simultaneously raising their lips to display blood-stained gums and teeth... just in case he got it into his mind that escape might still be possible.

* * *

THE POLICE EVENTUALLY ARRIVED; detailed statements were taken. However, it was agreed beforehand between the Taylor and Galbraith families that there be no mention of the history leading up to that day's events, or of stolen gold, or of any previous knowledge of Teddy Green: to just explain things as a random house break-in, by an unknown, seriously demented and desperate individual.

Teddy was taken away in a sad, disoriented mental state, hands cuffed behind his back, his voice mostly incoherent and his repeated nonsensical protests ignored.

Three months later a still very tormented Teddy passed away and was interred God only knows where.

* * *

'QUITE AN EVENTFUL DAY, one could say, though I suggest you should retire that shotgun forever. However, my matey, should your circumstances ever change, you'll probably need this,' said Patrick as he tossed a tiny pocketknife to Harry.

'Yeah, thanks. Robert's trusty pocketknife. I wondered where that got to. And look, it's a bit rusty, but it still has his initials etched on the biggest blade... RWE, if I'm not mistaken.

'More importantly though Patrick, what will our boys think of *me* now?'

'I wouldn't worry yourself, my friend; I've told them all about you, warts an' all. You'll always be their hero, Harry!'

'Yeah, but will they believe I missed that bastard, or that I deliberately missed because I didn't want to shoot someone in the back who was also unarmed?'

'That's water under the bridge now, Harry. Forget it and let's crack open another bottle. You do feel like a beer, I suppose?'

'Nah, not just now, later perhaps. I'd rather go up the park and have a kick of the footy with our boys. You want to come?'

'Yeah, why not?'

'Hang about, you two,' cried Jane, 'Harry darling, I've had a bit too much excitement for today... you'll first have to get me to hospital, before I burst.'

THE END

AN EXPLANATORY NOTE

Throughout this novel, my principal objective was to maintain its plot and storyline in lockstep with the timeline of Australia's recorded history. However, the reader may have spotted some chronological irregularities, resulting from the need for authorial licence to complete this story's evolving timeline.

This account is, to some extent, a story of sentiment regarding how our first nation people were so sadly unrecognised and so unjustly treated, and how, not all the unreported immoral actions perpetrated upon them were left unpunished.

On balance, our bushrangers, too, left a lot to be desired. Though their circumstances often drove them to wrongdoings, their subsequent actions frequently reflected a sense of justice.

This book is a novel; occasionally uncovering evil and at times tinted with humour, but on balance, hopefully you found it a thought-provoking read.

ACKNOWLEDGMENTS

Dr Bob Rich.

My masterful mentor: renowned author of 20+ remarkable books, always available to help, always encouraging. A truly amazing Australian and friend. Again, thanks heaps, Bob.

Tony Park.

Internationally renowned Australian/Zimbabwean author and entrepreneur. I greatly appreciated your mateship, down-to-earth mentorship and encouragement while attending your highly successful, June 2022, "Writer's Safari" at Nantwich.

And, never to be forgotten, your patient, amazing assistance in providing new commercial pathways enabling the publication and distribution of my work.

Jo-Anne Richards.

Can't imagine anyone more suited to teaching creative writing! Jo-Anne is a South African novelist whose work has been published internationally. Thanks for your unrelenting passion and good humour to ensure my writing endeavours can succeed. Your workshop deliveries while lecturing at the June 2022 Writers Safari, at Nantwich, were absorbing and great fun.

Those participants who attended the June 2022 "Writer's Safari" hosted by Tony Park at his Nantwich lodge, in the Harare National Park, Zimbabwe.

I won't list them here, but they will know who I'm referring to should they read this book.

A truly amazing, talented group of folks. Unwittingly, I suspect, they probably have no idea how beneficial their interjections, suggestions and joyful exchanges have so profoundly influenced my authorial thoughts.

Yvonne Versteegen.

Thanks so much for your tireless and timely assistance in not only proofreading my manuscript, but for your meaningful editorial recommendations.

TREVOR TUCKER

Inspired by the joy and intense satisfaction of writing my first three books, "*Ned Kelly's Son*", "*The Stolen maps... Australia's greatest maritime secret?*" *and* "*Aussie Anecdotes*"... plus the success of their sales, I embarked upon my fourth authorial adventure.

A Sense of Justice was inspired by the thought of witnessing life on the outskirts of recorded history and suggesting alternative feasible outcomes, albeit not as historians conjectured.

I have now formed the belief that writing is a most satisfying outlet for creativity... both challenging, and relaxing. However, writing is not just escapism, but rather the compulsion of a glorious illness, that which I call, **The Dreamer's Disease**, i.e., that the more you give, the more you receive.

Having retired from the oil and gas industry, my other interests include when possible, spending time with my kids, and grandkids, fishing, reading, bike riding, watching Test cricket and AFL football (in both men's and women's formats), and listening to classical music... but most of all, enjoying the life-changing experiences of travelling the world.

A whiff of speculation still surrounds much of Australia's colonial history

The documented lives of some notorious characters and certain historical events are not always as irrefutably correct (or complete) as many historians would like us to believe. Most historians, however, have produced excellent representations based upon thousands of hours (years, even) of painstaking research, but they have not always presented "the complete story"... hinting that some of their records are likely to reveal "a captivating twist in the final telling".

Arguably, the most frustrating example of this has arisen after the shootout between the Kelly Gang and the Victorian police, at Glenrowan in 1880. The aftermath of that event remains clouded because of the reluctance of locals to take up the pen at that time to record what they had witnessed, for fear of police reprisals either upon themselves or upon their neighbours.

Since the settlement of Australia, two incontestable facts remain. First, that verifiable written record has always been very thin on the ground. Second, the privacy of unrecorded witness accounts of some unwaveringly loyal folk was assured when they were assigned to their graves.

Ongoing investigation may yet uncover pertinent facts that will add certainty to Australian historical record. For example, DNA evidence now (apparently) exists that Dan Kelly—of Ned Kelly Gang infamy and thought to have been burnt to a crisp during the Glenrowan shootout—actually lived for decades in a remote town, in south central Queensland, and was buried there.

But this story is not another "Kelly Gang story"!

It is, if you have read this far, the story of two previously unknown men; unlikely thieves, heroes possibly, who roamed the vastness of Australia and unintentionally found themselves immersed in the periphery of some significant events that shaped Australia during the nineteenth century... and portrays their sense of justice.

READER REVIEWS

Reader Reviews

Trevor Tucker's specialty is fictional accounts of Australia's early history, but so well researched that one wonders how much of it is his invention.

In this volume, we follow the lives of two men: one with authority, the scion of a wealthy family, the other transported to what would one day become Australia as a convict. His "crime" was to remove an otherwise useless offcut of timber from a building site so he could make a coffin for his father.

You can follow the many twists of fate that have them team up and become very interested in illegally acquiring a fortune.

Do they?

Do they get away with it?

You'll need to read the story to find out.

Dr Bob Rich. *A self-proclaimed professional grandfather, author of 20+ thought provoking and helpful books and a retired "life coach and counsellor". Bob's main motivation continues to be to transform society to create a sustainable world in which his grandchildren and their grandchildren in perpetuity can have a life, and a life worth living.*

Trevor, you've done it again! History, ethical dilemmas, action and excitement, building towards the grand finale. A great read and thoroughly enjoyable.

Yve Versteegen. *Gym instructress extraordinaire. Lilydale, Victoria.*

Excellent and captivating story that is very thought provoking on the injustices to First Nations peoples. Trevor's style of storytelling transports you back in time to such an extent you can vividly picture the scenery of early Australia.

Jane Carroll. *Former fraud Intelligence Analyst, now Carer/retiree of the "Chateau on Tambo Retreat" at Swifts Creek in Gippsland, Victoria.*